TAG THE REDEMPTION

A WOLF SHIFTER FATED MATES PARANORMAL ROMANCE

BILLIONAIRE WOLVES SERIES
BOOK THREE

CHARMAINE LOUISE SHELTON

CONTENTS

WANT FREE BOOKS?

Want to know what happened to Jagger's best friend Dylan? Find out in *Dylan The Rogue: A Wolf Shifter Fated Mates Paranormal Romance* your FREE Book!

Click Cover Below or visit **bit.ly/ CLBooksDylanTheRogue** to subscribe to my newsletter for latest news and launches, books from my author friends, and sizzling reads in book promotions. Plus, start reading the steamy fated mates romance for bad boy wolf shifter Dylan.

ABOUT TAG THE REDEMPTION: A WOLF SHIFTER FATED MATES PARANORMAL ROMANCE

What havoc can my shy, curvaceous human assistant wreak on my structured life? Drive my wolf feral.

As the beta of my wolf pack—the Billionaire Wolves of Miami—and the COO of our multibillion-dollar corporation, I demand control and order in my life. A serious wolf shifter with no time for drama or a relationship. They don't call me Mr. Grumpy and bosshole for nothing. But the gods have other plans when they choose Wren Byrd as my fated mate. The BBW personifies chaos. But my wolf wants her. Despite the ring on her finger.

All my life others teased me for being more robust and for not wearing a size zero. I'm curvy, darn it! So, when Jonathan the hot man of my dreams proposes, I accept. Then catch him with his sassy and slim neighbor. I accept his forgiveness—who else wants me? Until I meet Tag

Dahl, my new boss. The beast of a male sets my soul on fire.

Little do I know he's not all he seems. And Jonathan won't accept he lost. He means to ruin my life…

Their steamy love story is a standalone in the sizzling **Billionaire Wolves Series** *of interconnecting stories featuring wolf shifter fated mates romance. Get a glimpse of their dynamism in other books.*

Anthem: "Live Your Life" T.I. featuring Rihanna
https://www.youtube.com/watch?v=koVHN6eO4Xg

Visit CharmaineLouiseBooks.com

CHAPTER 1

WHY DO they whisper I'm a bosshole? Case in point...

"And that concludes the marketing department's promotion plan for the new build in Naples."

A hush descends in the conference room as fifteen pairs of eyes peek nervously at me. I keep mine laser focused on the male wolf shifter who heads the marketing team for the Naples residential project. He lowers his gaze respectfully as he awaits my comments.

As the COO of Larson Enterprises, Inc. it's my responsibility to manage and to handle the day-to-day business operations of the Miami Wolves Pack's multibillion-dollar company. Including working closely with department heads and supervisors to support the daily activity of employees.

A lot of pieces must move in sync to maintain Larson Enterprises as the top company in the hospitality industry for luxury hotels, fine dining, clubs, and lounges. Founded in Miami by our pack Alpha's family—with Jagger Larson as the current CEO. I'm his second in command as COO and as his pack beta. Both roles I take very seriously.

So much so that I will not tolerate less than stellar work by staff. And that means I have to hold back an irritated growl at the half-ass *promotion plan* presented. I'm surprised the male bothered. He should have known better. And I don't hesitate to express my dissatisfaction. At. All.

"Do you truly expect me to believe you did your research, Jackson?!" I bark, then hold up my hand when he opens his mouth to respond. "Rhetorical question. Obviously, you did *not*. Otherwise, you would recall a similar 'promotion plan' presented three months ago. One I rejected. The same I do with this one. You have twenty-four hours. I expect an *original* plan on my desk."

"Yes, Mr. Dahl, sir," he responds, then slinks to his seat.

As he hovers above it with his hands on the armrests, I shake my head with several tsks. His startled eyes jump to mine. I cock my head.

"Don't you think you should gather your team now? You have your work cut out for you, Jackson."

He stutters a response as he hops up and dashes towards the double doors.

I watch him go, then flick my gaze to the head of business development.

"Sally."

The human female swallows audibly, bobbing her head as she rises.

"Yes, Mr. Dahl, sir."

I sit forward, lean my elbows on the sleek conference table, and steeple my fingers. Next…

Two hours later, I stride past the staff on the executive floor on my way to my suite of offices. We employ wolf shifters and humans. Best for our kind to hide in plain sight and all. Although we've been here a hell of a lot longer than the humans.

Several millennia ago, Scandinavian Viking wolf shifters sailed from the Old World and landed along the East Coast of what's now the United States. The six packs headed by best friends who sought new lands moved throughout the continent to form territories, with ours settling here. We maintain close ties with our brethren through friendship, mating, and business. Plus, our Ruling Council gatherings keep us informed of happenings throughout the packs.

Our Miami Wolves Pack is the most powerful pack in the South. Because of the success of Larson Enterprises, other packs refer to us as the *Billionaire Wolves of Miami.* Further reason for me to ensure I fulfill my responsibility to take Jagger's CEO vision for the company and turn it into an executable business plan. Correction, a *flawless* executable business plan. So, call me bosshole all day. And sometimes all night.

I round the corner to my office suite and nod at my administrative assistant, Beth. The she-wolf scampers to her feet from behind her desk outside my office and hands a file folder to me. Her head tilts back since I tower over her at six feet seven inches.

"Here's your speech for the charity gala tonight, Mr. Dahl. Communications made your requested edits, sir."

"Thank you, Beth. My date is aware of the time I'll pick her up?"

"Yes, Mr. Dahl. I spoke with Katrina an hour ago. She confirms she will be ready. Your lunch delivery is on its way up now. Both Mr. Larsons, Dr. Ingolf, and Mr. Vang wait in your office."

I figured as much since the opaque treatment blocks the clear glass wall. Jagger must have activated it knowing we'd want privacy for our weekly Guys' Lunch. Today it's my turn. Naturally, I'm hosting it here in between meetings.

More than likely, I'll hear about it from them since I'm always in the office. So what? Unlike Jagger and Dylan, I don't have—nor do I want—a mate that keeps me tethered to her side. Or like Viggo, who can't stay out of any female's panties. Rust is the only one as tied to his job as I am to mine. He's in the emergency room as a critical care surgeon more than anyplace else. Inwardly, I shrug. Outwardly, I nod at my assistant.

"Thank you, Beth. You may leave for your lunch early."

"Thank you, Mr. Dahl."

I open the double doors of my office. My best friends lounge on the white leather sofa and chairs in the sitting area with their feet up on the coffee table and armrests guffawing. Thank the gods my office is obscured and soundproof with this lot.

We've been friends since we were pups. My father Branson was the enforcer for the former Alpha Marcus—Jagger's father. Jagger and I were born a few weeks apart and inseparable for twenty-eight years. My mother Ylva teases the former Luna Sigrid she stole her only pup. Rust Ingolf and Dylan Vang are a year older, while Viggo came along two years later as Jagger's younger brother. The five of us share a strong bond as best friends, even going so far as to get wolf paw tattoos on our pecs. Well, Jagger wussed out, claiming he has no interest in marring his perfect body. Regardless, we treat each other like blood brothers. And that includes getting on my nerves kicking back on my furniture with no care whatsoever…

"Hello, gentlemen. A pleasure, as always."

They pivot as one pack. Heads cock. Eyes sharp. Nostrils flare. Then the grins spread across their faces, laughing at the scowl on my face as my eyes flick between their feet and the furniture.

"Why hello there, Mr. Grumpy!"

"How's your grumpilicious day going, bro?"

"Why the sour face? Don't you love us anymore?"

"I hope your status meeting went better than the expression on your face…"

I shake my head as I loosen my silk tie and shrug out of

my bespoke suit jacket. Oh, yeah, we're all billionaires, and they're dressed in similar high-end apparel. Young, sexy AF, and wealthy beyond our wildest dreams.

"Hello. Again. My day would be better without your boots on my white leather sofa. I can't get rid of you, so I'm forced to love you. Other than a wreck of a promo plan, the meeting went well, surprisingly."

A knock on the door cuts into their uproarious chuckles. I stride over and open it. Beth leads the delivery person to the conference table beside the floor-to-ceiling wall of windows.

As they arrange the gourmet meals from a Larson restaurant at each chair, I glance at the view always captivated by the stunning panorama. One of the tallest buildings in the city, The Larson Tower in Downtown Miami Bayfront stands seventy-five floors high across from Biscayne Bay. Beyond its azure waters—where jet skiers zip by and megayachts cruise along—lies the Atlantic Ocean. Its dazzling turquoise surface extends to the horizon as far as the eye can see. I inhale and relax. The clamoring of the guys as they pull out chairs and check who has what food interrupts my all too brief respite. I roll my eyes and drop into a white leather executive chair.

We shoot the shit about the latest Miami Dolphins football game, Viggo's new blinged out watch, and our upcoming deep-sea fishing trip to the Bahamas. My mobile vibrates in my pocket. I groan at the photos on the screen.

"What's up?" Rust asks as he peers over my shoulder. He barks out a laugh. "For real? You've gotta be kidding me!"

He snatches my mobile and passes it to Dylan, who guffaws and passes it to Viggo and on to Jagger. Until I grab it back with a growl, emerald green eyes flash with my displeased wolf.

"What the hell is Katrina up to?"

I sigh and run my fingers through the short length of my sable brown hair.

"She's accompanying me to the charity gala tonight. I thought she behaved well at the hotel opening last week and figured she'd be a suitable candidate for another social event. Obviously, she thought more of the invitation."

Dylan chuckles and smirks.

"You don't say? If the lingerie pics under the guise of 'Which, do you prefer?' didn't clue you in, I don't know what would!"

I groan and respond with a terse not interested and no need to get dressed at all since you won't join me, then toss my mobile on the table.

I'm no monk. I like to fuck. A lot. But I keep my life segmented by work, social events, and sex and keep the participants separated. The luxury, members-only BDSM lifestyle club on Ocean Drive—Club Sol & Mani Miami— owned by our pack provides me with willing she-wolf submissives to satisfy my Alpha Dominant kinks. And even there, I play with several subs. I never let the thought of one being a favorite form in their heads. So, no, I don't need lingerie photos of Katrina. She lost her spot in the social events segment for good. But now, who to take I ponder as my head shakes.

Viggo studies me with ice blue eyes so like his brother's but has fiery copper red hair. I cock my head at the younger wolf shifter.

"Why don't you hire another assistant who can manage your social calendar and attend events with you? As an employee, she won't expect to become Mrs. Tag Dahl. Better yet, hire a human female. Then it's zero chance of her thinking she's your mate. We may fuck a human female. But it's been decades since a male wolf shifter turned a human in our pack. No wrong ideas or vavavavoom photos!"

He snaps his fingers and sits back, arms crossed over his muscular chest. A triumphant grin appears on his face.

I stare at him.

A human female assistant to handle my personal affairs with no endgame to mate with me? No coy smiles or hair flips? Actual conversations and not double entendres? A business professional who expects a paycheck and not a diamond rock? Well, damn! Let me contact Human Resources right now.

A grin spreads across my face as the idea settles in.

"Hell yeah, Viggo! That's just what I need. In fact, I'll email the head of HR—"

My mobile skitters across the smooth surface of the table like a hockey puck. Dylan's massive mitts catch it as he grins at Jagger.

"Not now, you're not. You're having lunch with your best friends. Work can wait," Jagger says with a smirk. "And

I'm telling you that as Alpha, CEO, and best friend. No room for dispute or negotiation, bro."

I roll my eyes and sit back.

These guys are lucky I do love them. Or else I'd kick their asses.

"Now that you dumped Katrina, who will you take?"

I shrug in answer to Rust's question.

After seeing the she-wolf's unwanted photos, I'd rather go alone. Although, having a female on my arm keeps others at bay. Well, for the most part. I've had a few approach me the moment my date stepped away to the ladies' room. I may be a bosshole. But I'm still a gentleman and made it clear I was with someone. Tonight, I won't be in the mood to dodge hopeful females.

"Take Signy. The social princess is always up for an event if her calendar allows a last-minute engagement. Give her a reason to wear one of her beloved haute couture gowns."

Viggo's suggestion pulls me from my musings. His and Jagger's younger sister is the pack princess and a little sister to me. So, again, no chance for mistaken expectations. Perfect!

"Damn, bro, you're on fire today, huh?" Dylan teases with a smirk. "Trying to get Brownie points or what?"

Viggo throws a handful of French fries across the table in response. Herbs and Parmesan cheese crumbles drop to the surface. Dylan picks the fries up and pops them in his mouth.

I growl, and they laugh.

"Listen, I'm not due to the ER for another few hours. I have no interest in saving either of your asses from Tag's wrath. So, cut the shit," Rust says as he eyes them.

Dylan grabs him in a headlock and noogies his head.

I refuse to play referee—or preschool teacher—and ignore them. Instead, I snag my mobile to call Signy.

"IT NEVER CEASES to amaze me how well you scrub up. I remember you as a pup chasing behind your brothers and the guys to prove you're just as tough."

Signy rolls her ice blue eyes as I tease her.

She's a gorgeous she-wolf and dressed spectacularly in a signature red Valentino haute couture gown with a matching clutch and strappy stilettos. Her waist-long ebony hair piled atop her head in an easy bun and blood red lipstick offer contrast to the elegant gown. Ruby and diamonds sparkle on her ears, neck, finger, and at both wrists. An absolute stunner.

Which is exactly why her brothers and the rest of us run interference with any male who dares to get close to Signy. Only the best and the most worthy male will court the pack princess. At twenty-four, she has plenty of time before she mates. Not that she has a choice. Especially since Jagger nixed the attempt by an Alpha from out west to claim her.

"Tag, that was decades ago! Now, come on or, we'll be late, Mr. I Have an Overseas Call I Can't Skip."

She loops her arm through mine and drags me towards the front doors of the bayfront mansion she lives in with her parents. I help her into the back of my chauffeured Bentley Bentayga and round the back to slide in beside her. An enforcer for the pack serves as my driver and personal security, along with a second enforcer who rides in the passenger seat.

She bleeds my ear about her latest exploits—social events attended, philanthropic work—pack gossip, and her next trip to Europe for fashion week. I indulge her like a good older brother, even though my mind drifts to my business trip.

"—And the cow jumped over the moon."

I frown and lift an eyebrow at her. She shakes her head.

"You weren't listening to a word I said, Tag. Let me guess, you have some important business on your mind?"

I open my mouth to protest, but she lifts her hand to stop me.

"That's why you need to take a hint from your boys and find your fated mate. Then you won't only have Larson Enterprises to occupy your mind."

Thankfully, the luxury SUV stops in front of the Larson Miami Hotel & Resort, saving me from responding. Without a word, I hop out and stride around to her side. The enforcer holds her door open while I extend my arm. She places a dainty hand on my forearm as a brilliant smile spreads across her face.

Immediately, cameras flash from the paparazzi covering the charity gala for local society papers and websites to national and international media outlets. They call Signy's name since she's a regular on the social scene.

She alights from the luxury SUV with grace. Her gown flows behind her as I escort her down the red carpet. She's a beauty amidst the other patrons lined up for photos or chatting with the camera crews. We pause in front of the step and repeat where the Larson Enterprises, Inc. logo blazes behind her. She smiles and points at it with a red-polished, manicured fingernail. The paparazzi go wild. The flashes blinding. I stand aside and respond to emails on my mobile.

A tug on my arm alerts me to Signy's return to my side. I smile, and we head inside for the rooftop ballroom with an outdoor terrace. The night goes as planned. We mingle with others during the cocktail hour. Females know better than to approach me with Signy on my arm. Her eyes flash if they come anywhere near me. I send my thanks to Viggo.

After my speech and dinner, Signy wants to get some air. Although I think she has her eye on a particular human male. Like I'll let that happen. But again, I indulge her.

We step through the opening created by the wall of glass sliding into side pockets. Others have the same idea of enjoying the evening breeze off the Atlantic Ocean, creating a glitzy crowd of designer gowns and tuxedos. Their laughter and the buzz of conversations float all around.

I glance at my Patek Philippe timepiece. Another thirty minutes, and we're out. I let Signy guide me in the direction the human male took.

I stop, stunned.

Eyes narrow. Nostrils flare. Cock thickens. A rumble grows in my chest. The urge to howl grips my throat. I inhale deeply.

Carried on the breeze across the rooftop, the faint scent of cinnamon sugar caramel apples wafts towards me. The unique scent I inhaled as my first breath when born tantalizes my senses. The scent of the only she-wolf destined for me.

My fated mate.

 *ren*

"Hello… Earth to Wren Byrd… Come back to the room, chica."

I blink to clear my unfocused gaze and turn to my personal trainer turned best friend, Maya Alejandra Perez Garcia. Her jet black eyebrows knit together over her expressive topaz eyes. Looking at her gorgeous face makes my thoughts wander again to last night's unpleasant encounter.

Maya is everything I'm not. A former fitness model with proportionate curves whose body makes men fall at her feet. Five inches taller than me at five feet, nine inches. Not to mention her confident, outgoing, and independent personality. The only commonality is our age of twenty-five. Gee…

Her eyes narrow as they scan my face. Undoubtedly, the misery from last night appears on its fullness. She places her hands on her hips and arches an eyebrow.

"Spill it, Wren. What happened?"

My eyes slink away as I shrug. Instead of responding, I head to the treadmill for my warm-up before our training session begins. I ignore the panorama of Biscayne Bay out to the Atlantic Ocean while my fingers fiddle with the digital display panel. The treadmill belt starts slowly.

"Oh, no you won't," Maya says as she slams her palm on the big red stop button. I grip the side rails and glance at her. "Before we begin, we need to clear your head so you can focus on yourself and not on whatever upset you. This way."

I follow her to the corner of the gym on the top floor of my luxury condo building in Brickell. She rolls two large stability balls to the floor-to-ceiling windows. The expanse of the glass allows the brilliant Miami sun to shine on us as we settle on the balls. I wobble before I find my balance.

Maya sits with ease and flicks her long ponytail over her shoulder, bare in a white crop bra. She rests her hands on her lithe thighs covered in the matching leggings. Her expectant gaze focuses on me. Obviously, there's no chance to avoid an answer.

I adjust my black t-shirt over my soft belly. My palms slide along the black joggers. All black everything, I mean, it's the best color to cover flaws, right? Inwardly, I roll my eyes. Outwardly, I sigh. Might as well get this over with.

At least Maya is my best friend and won't judge me. She'll definitely have loads to say after she finishes cursing in Spanish. I wince at the thought. Fortunately, the gym is empty now. No one to overhear me recount the disastrous night. Ugh!

"I caught Jonathan with his neighbor."

My hot fiancé with his sassy and slim neighbor—again my complete opposite—to be exact. Last night when I arrived at his condo to surprise him with dinner from his favorite restaurant, the front door was ajar. Concerned, I pushed it open and crept inside, not wanting to alert an intruder to my presence. When, in fact, *I* was the intruder.

My jaw dropped when I found him not in an uncompromising position with a home invader. But in one with his blonde neighbor who always makes snide comments about me or wrinkles her nose at the sight of me. Of course, Jonathan says I'm being overly sensitive and imagining things. But them in the living room with her naked on her knees between his spread legs and her head bobbing while his leans back against the pillow was no figment of my imagination.

In my haste to get away, I backed into the wall and knocked a painting to the floor. Their heads jerked in my direction. His eyes widened while hers gleamed. She even had the audacity to lick her puffy lips. I covered my mouth and spun on my heels, dropping the bag with dinner. Jonathan calling my name as the sound of him scrambling to his feet spurred me on. I reached the door and ran down the hallway to the elevators. Frantically, I pressed the call button. The blasted doors didn't open before he caught up to me.

Shirtless and adjusting the erection that tented the front of his joggers, Jonathan grabbed my elbow and hauled me to his condo. I tried to pull back, but he was determined. The neighbor slipped out his door with a maxi dress now covering her slim figure. Jonathan ignored her and turned his back. She winked at me before she sashayed towards her door. Tears blurred the vision of her trim hips swaying.

"For fuck's sake, don't get so emotional, Wren. It's not what you think."

I pulled my arm from his grasp and glared through my tears.

"Oh, really? My fiancé's manhood in the mouth of another woman should not upset me? Is that what you're saying, Jonathan? Seriously?"

He scrubbed a hand down his face and murmured what sounded like *at least it was in someone's mouth.*

I choked back a sob and spun around for the door. His audible words stopped me.

"Wren, she means nothing to me. I lost an important client today. Cassie stopped by for a screwdriver and one thing led to another. I just had to let go of the frustrations. You know your uncle. He was beyond pissed."

Uncle George—the CEO of Byrd Capital, our family's financial company, and my late father's older brother. My guardian since my parents, Ethan and Connie, died in a boating accident sixteen years ago. More like I'm his burden. He happily introduced me to Jonathan to marry me off to a man who can take me off his list of responsibilities and who can run the company when he retires. Naturally, Uncle George doesn't believe a woman can man the helm of our family's business. Despite me being the sole heir since he's unable to have children with my Aunt Gretchen—rather, Wretched Gretchen—he prefers an outsider. And I know from experience how angry he can get when disappointed.

I folded my arms across my middle.

Jonathan took it as a sign I was caving in and placed his hands on my shoulders. At six feet, he bent his knees to align our gazes. He fixed me with an intense stare as his turquoise blue eyes met my mink brown ones.

Before he speaks, I cut in.

"She came to borrow a screwdriver or to get screwed? Which is it, Jonathan, since it certainly appeared the latter to me!"

He had the good grace to flinch but shook it off. His blond hair—longer on the top—tumbled over his forehead. He gave me his signature hot hunk smile—the same one I fell for when Uncle George introduced us two years ago.

Jonathan was more than elated to meet me. At the time, he was doing well with the company. The son of Uncle George's friend from Harvard University and a family close in social ranking to ours. Uncle George sees it as a power match. I see it as a hot guy who's attracted to me—for once. Six months ago, he proposed, and I accepted. Now, my uncle grooms Jonathan for the CEO role. Meanwhile, I'm a socialite and the dutiful fiancée. Boring!

"Come on now, Wren. You have to believe me. Cassie means nothing. What she did meant nothing. You're the only girl for me, babe. And I'm the only guy for you. You know that, don't you?"

He didn't wait for my response. Instead, he planted a chaste kiss on the top of my head as he stood and squeezed my shoulders. A glance behind put a smile on his handsome face.

"Wow! That smells like food from STK Steakhouse. What a pleasant surprise. Thanks, babe. I'm starving!" Jonathan said as he sauntered past me to the bag I had dropped. Confident I'm pacified, he put the horrible situation behind him with ease.

I turned and watched his taut butt flex beneath the cotton joggers. He's right. He is the "only guy for me." What other hottie would want a chubby like me for a wife? None.

I sighed then and sigh now as I finish my sorry story.

Maya's topaz eyes flashed throughout. Now, she jumps to her feet and curses as she storms around the gym. Fluent in Spanish, I nod along glum until she grabs my hands and yanks me to my feet. Did I mention she's strong?

"Wren, you've come so far in your confidence level. Remember, you are so much more than you give yourself credit for. You're worthy of a man who loves you, respects you, and would end the world for you! Do. Not. Settle. For. Less!"

Maya's impassioned response brings tears to my eyes. I can only nod, too emotional to speak.

"You know, I think you should dump his cheating ass. But I will support you no matter what you decide. However, I will not allow you to let his trifling behavior derail your wellbeing progress!"

She squeezes my hands and nods towards the gym's bathroom.

"Go rinse your face with cool water. We have work to do, chica!"

"WREN, did we not decide you should wear the black ballgown with three-quarter sleeves and high neckline? What are you doing in that flashy dress?"

Wretched Gretchen's midnight blue eyes would widen if she didn't have Botox injections regularly. Instead, she blinks rapidly. One auburn eyebrow twitches slightly, unable to arch.

Regardless of her nature, my aunt looks elegant as always. This time in a goldenrod-colored strapless pleated silk-faille gown. The column silhouette with voluminous, draped panels that skim the sides pool at the floor accentuates her tall, willowy figure. The folded neckline and gathered waist add to its sculptural feel. Makeup and hair coiffed to perfection. Diamonds drip from her ears, neck, and wrists. She's regal.

However, I'm no slouch with the gown Maya helped me to select instead of the frumpy one Wretched Gretchen advised. *It will hide those not so pleasant parts of your physique, Wren, dear.*

The gown skims my BBW figure—as Maya calls it—and ends in a fishtail hem that cascades to the floor. Crystals form a pattern to mimic a chandelier on the moss green stretch silk jersey. Thin straps at the shoulders dip to a v-neckline offer a glimpse of my full breasts. Thanks to the Spandex Goddess, I'm nice and sleek.

Strappy sandals add five inches to my five feet, four inches. A colorful crystal minaud in the shape of a butterfly rests in my palm. Minimal makeup and my mahogany hair falling in lush waves to the middle of my back complete my look.

I lift my chin proudly as I respond to Wretched Gretchen.

"*You* decided the black ballgown. However, *I* prefer this one."

My heart hammers in my chest as I wait for her response.

When she and Uncle George brought me into their home at nine, I was a regular-sized child. But the grief of losing my parents caused me to withdraw. I sought solace in food. The resulting weight gain drove my aunt to put me on every diet known to man. They worked for a time. But I hid snacks in my room and ate late at night after they went to bed. At weigh-ins, she couldn't understand the lack of weight loss and the increase of pounds. Until she found cookies in my backpack. Her steely gaze sent shudders through me. Even now.

She scrutinizes me from head to toe as she circles me like a bird of prey. Stopping in front of me, her lips form a ruby slash on her stunning face.

"Well, at least you left your hair out. I've always said it's your best asset, Wren, dear."

"All right. Let's get going. We don't want to be late."

Wretched Gretchen and I turn to Uncle George's booming voice. He and Jonathan enter the living room. When he and I arrived at my uncle and aunt's oceanfront mansion on Fisher Island, Jonathan went to the study, saying he had to discuss something with Uncle George.

I've never been happier to see them. Relieved to avoid further scrutiny, I pivot and head for the front doors.

"Wren, what the hell do you have on?!"

Well, maybe not…

As the limousine slides in front of the Larson Miami Hotel & Resort, I don't wait for the valet to open the door. Eager to escape the thick fog of tension, I push the door open into his hand, then nod in thanks as he helps me from the limo. Jonathan emerges after me and takes my elbow. He's all smiles for the flashing cameras on the red carpet.

The charity gala is a big event on Miami elite's social calendar. I'm sure he expects to make business connections with the wealthy guests. Whatever.

Drawing on Maya's words, I straighten my spine and

force a smile onto my face. Regardless of the naysayers, I will do my best to embrace being a BBW.

The verdict is still out on my relationship with Jonathan. I only came tonight to avoid questions from Uncle George and Wretched Gretchen. I do not wish to disclose what happened to them. At. All.

We make it through the cocktail hour, mingling with others. Jonathan takes every opportunity to inform people he's with Byrd Capital, and I'm his fiancée, Wren Byrd. They smile politely. Some women give me the once-over for having a hunk. But I ignore the flutter of self-doubt gnawing in my belly.

I'm surprised by Jonathan's attentiveness. He's portraying the perfect fiancé despite last night's fiasco. I shudder at the memory of him bowing out, claiming an early morning meeting when I cuddled up next to him on the sofa after we ate. I nodded, not wanting him to notice how much he wounded me. He was all ready for his neighbor. But me… Not so much.

"Wren?"

I blink out of my musings at the sound of his voice.

"It's time to move into the ballroom for dinner. I'm sure you're ready to eat."

Now, I blink to hold back tears. However, Jonathan turns towards the doors and misses my reaction. I will the tears away and let him lead me to the tables. Just a while longer, and I'll make an excuse to leave.

I rely on the social skills imprinted on my brain from the moment my uncle and my aunt became my guardians.

He didn't want me to embarrass him in any way. So, the table conversation flows. After dinner, the couple on Jonathan's left announce they're going onto the outdoor terrace for cordials.

"Come on, they're brilliant prospects," he murmurs in my ear, then stands and helps me from my chair.

I nod around the table at the others. They return the parting gesture.

Half listening to Jonathan gush about the couple's potential to save his lost deal, I plan my escape. Once outside, I accept a proffered cordial from a server and take a sip.

"Oh, my," I say as I hold back from Jonathan. He glances over his shoulder at me. I frown and shake my head. "I—I don't feel so well. It's best if I leave. Now."

He scowls then turns to the couple a few feet ahead of us.

"Really, Wren? Didn't I just say the guy's company would make up for the deal I lost? I can't leave now," Jonathan says, fully irked by my sudden illness. There goes the attentive fiancé.

I shake my head and pat his arm.

"No. You stay. I'll have Uncle George's driver take me home. They won't need the limo any time soon. And don't you worry about me. I'll make it out of here without your help."

Jonathan graces me with his hot hunk smile, completely oblivious to my sarcasm. Poor thing.

"Great! I'll call you tomorrow."

I watch as he rushes to the couple. The man has his arm around the woman's waist, leaning close to her ear. Their cheeks press together. She giggles and cups his face. The love they share is clear on their cheerful faces.

Now, why can't I find a man who will stare at me like I'm his moon and stars and not scowl like I'm a pesky burden?

 *ren*

"You know, I was thinking about what you said about reducing your dependence on your uncle. A client told me about a job opening at her company, Larson Enterprises, Inc. She's in the Human Resources department and learned the COO wants a social assistant. Someone who can help him with his social calendar, like scheduling events, coordinating functions, and attending them with him. Yada, yada, yada. I thought about you since that's your thing, Ms. Socialite. She said the salary was pretty high for the position. The COO wants someone he can trust and knows her stuff. Not someone who will look for a big fat diamond ring. He's a sexy as sin billionaire, by the way. I looked him up."

Maya giggles.

We finished an outdoor session in the park next to Biscayne Bay and went across the street to Pura Vida for açaí bowls. Sitting on the open field of grass surrounded by palm trees blowing in the balmy breeze, the morning sun shines on us, making her topaz eyes sparkle. I grin back.

The thought of a job that pays me enough I won't need to rely on Uncle George's monthly allotment and makes me responsible for myself fills my heart with happiness. I could prove I'm capable and not flighty like my father. Never do I think of my Dad in that way.

But Uncle George rarely lets a day go by he doesn't remind me how disappointed he is in my father not taking his place at Byrd Capital. He thinks my father wasted his life and married beneath the family. Even my name irks Uncle George. *Wren Byrd. Bird Bird. Such a silly name!*

Silly or not, it's my name. One of the few things I still have from my parents.

Uncle George told me I was to begin my new life with him and Wretched Gretchen fresh. *Leave that nonsense your father instilled in you and whatever he gave you behind.* At nine, saddened by the loss of my parents, and unable to stand up for myself, I had no choice but to obey his command. My name, memories, and photo albums survived. I cherish them. Even now, my heart clenches. I miss my parents constantly.

A chance to get from under Uncle George's control would be a win. I'll use all the etiquette classes and event planning sessions he and Wretched Gretchen insisted I take part in. Social connections the Byrd name generates prove an added bonus. I'm on the list for invitations to the best galas, fundraisers, and intimate gatherings in Miami and beyond. I find it hilarious the very means to escape and to prove I can make my own way in life comes from them!

Laughter bubbles up. I let it tumble from between my upturned lips until tears leak from the corners of my eyes. I laugh even harder when Maya joins in. So thankful for her, I throw my arms around my best friend. After we catch our breath, I sit back.

"How do I apply?"

"Atta girl! I'll send a text message to my client right now," Maya says as she whips her mobile from her duffle bag.

I watch as her fingers fly over the mobile screen. She pauses, then grins and types some more. Eager to know what's being said, I peer over her shoulder. I can't make out much. So, I sit back and pull my knees to my chest. Please, oh, please, oh please! I chant inwardly until Maya drops her mobile back in the bag and grins at me with a thumbs up.

"You're all set for an interview tomorrow morning at nine. I texted the details to you. She's excited to meet you since I kind of name-dropped who you are and all. Gotta use what you got to get what you want, you know," Maya says with a wink. "I have back-to-back client sessions. After, I'll come to your condo. We'll pick the best outfit and hairstyle. Sounds good?"

I hug her again.

"Absolutely! Thanks so much, bestie!"

A hot guy in a tank top and stretch-shell shorts lopes over and drops next to her. She startles as he says, boo. With a wry look, Maya folds her arms across her full breasts and tells him he'll do ten extra burpees double-time. He groans and falls to his back with an arm over his face dramatically. His head tilts towards me, and he winks. We laugh at his antics.

I bid them goodbye as I gather the empty açaí bowls and my crossbody bag. So excited for the job, I all but skip away clicking my heels! I toss the bowls into the trash can and head to my car.

A smile spreads across my face as I near it. My most recent nod to the more confident me is my birthday present—a BMW i4 eDrive40, the electric Gran Coupe. Upon first glance, the mineral white metallic exterior is simple. However, on closer inspection behind the tinted windows, the red leather interior gives a glimpse of my budding sassiness. Plus, it's better for the environment.

Naturally, Uncle George called it a ridiculous waste of more than $70K for a car with a gaudy interior. I held my tongue as he signed off on the purchase with his AMEX Centurion Card. Then I giddily slid behind the wheel, just like I do now.

I close my eyes as my fingers tighten around the steering wheel.

"Wren Byrd, you will get this job, do well at it, and

prove to Uncle George you are more than capable of taking care of yourself. Live your life!"

Happy, I sing aloud the lyrics from my personal anthem playlist as the warm sun and breeze fill my car. At a red stoplight, a little girl in a car beside mine giggles as she watches me belting out Rihanna's lyrics from T.I.'s "Live Your Life." I grin at her and hope she never has to deal with controlling people. Ever. When the stoplight changes to green, I wave at her. She puts her palm on her window and smiles. A good sign. My heart soars higher.

I thank my condo building's valet as I step from my car and slip a tip into his hand with a smile. He thanks me with a nod and slides behind the wheel. I hurry to the lobby, eager to get upstairs. The doorman greets me with a tilt of his head. I smile my thanks and wave at the concierge who wishes me a good day. It certainly is one!

As always, the endless expanse of the Atlantic Ocean beyond the floor-to-ceiling windows of my living room takes my breath away. The view from the fifty-fourth floor of my condo can't get any better.

Virginia Key, Fisher Island, and Dodge Island appear between the Atlantic Ocean and Biscayne Bay as I walk through the oversized living room with buttery soft sand-colored leather sofas and chairs. The golden sand-colored floor tiles angle toward the wall of windows to draw me closer. Out on the terrace, my gaze drops to my uncle and aunt's oceanfront mansion on Fisher Island.

My heart races at the sight of where I spent most of my years growing up miserable. I close my eyes on a long inhalation, then open them at the same pace on the exhalation. Maya's deep cleansing breath technique clears the negativity.

"Live your life, Wren Byrd!" I exclaim as my hands clap and my curvy hips shimmy. "Time to shower, put together your résumé, and check out your closet for a killer interview outfit!"

Hours later, Maya arrives. She showers and changes into a t-shirt and yoga pants in the second bedroom suite. It's become her home away from home.

"Okay, show me what you got," she announces as she steps into the sitting room, where I wait for her to finish. I jump to my feet and take her hand.

She giggles as I drag her down the hallway to the third bedroom suite converted into a dressing room. It's one of the few Wretched Gretchen's suggestions I agree with since I have tons of formal attire, evening wear, handbags, shoes, and accessories, not to mention regular daywear. It might as well be a posh mini boutique on Manhattan's Fifth Avenue. However, I donate the worn-once designer gowns to fundraising auctions to benefit various charities. Uncle George can't call that wasteful!

"Nice options, Wren! I really like that yellow suit. It brings out the rich mahogany color of your hair if you wear it loose down your back. Oh! The belted midi dress is so feminine. Hmmm... You can never go wrong with my fellow Venezuelan, Ms. Carolina Herrera, you know..."

I grin wider than the Cheshire Cat as Maya makes her

way down the row of clothes. She has such an expert eye. I value her opinion.

"Well, you want to go for chic and confident with your appearance, giving the air of a wealthy socialite. One who knows her stuff. Can handle an Alpha billionaire boss," Maya says as she taps a manicured fingernail against her full lips. Her assessing gaze sweeps over the outfits slowly.

My grin stretches further when she points at the navy blue sheath with matching waist-length jacket.

"This is it, chica!" Maya exclaims. "With those stilettos and your hair loose. Just accent your eyes, leaving your lips with a subtle pink stain."

"Perfect! I'll carry my powder blue top-handle bag since it fits my résumé portfolio. Will you take a look at it? I want to be sure I missed nothing."

We chat while I put the other items away before heading to the den where I left my laptop. Maya gives some recommendations on my résumé, and I make the changes. With a flourish, I place five copies in the portfolio. Maya claps enthusiastically, then grins.

"Okay, I'm hungry. Let's order some sushi. We can catch up on our fave *Bling Empire*. I rescheduled my morning sessions so I can spend the night, then help you get ready."

"Thanks so much, bestie!" I say as I throw my arms around her for a big hug. "You're the best bestie a girl could ever want!"

We laugh as Maya pulls out her mobile and places our delivery order. I grab the flat-screen television remote and switch to Netflix, settling in for a fun night. Excited butterflies flutter in my belly. I can't wait to start my new job. The power of positive thinking—another of Maya's techniques—makes me smile happily. You've got this, Wren Byrd!

"WELL, Wren, you impressed my colleagues and me with your education at Harvard, your experience with not only attending significant galas, but organizing them, and with your willingness to work long hours and on the weekends as necessary.

"Mr. Dahl has high expectations for all of Larson Enterprises' employees, especially for those who work with him in a direct capacity. As his social assistant, you would work closely with him.

"However, I must emphasize the need to maintain complete professionalism at all times. Mr. Dahl has the need of a trusted employee, not of a female interested in using the unique working situation as a means to marriage. Am I clear?"

The Head of Human Resources pauses to peer at me. Her fathomless obsidian eyes reach into the very depths of my soul.

I agree, then force myself to sit still under her intense scrutiny. Again, it's something I learned because of Uncle George and can apply it towards me getting this job.

After an almost imperceptible nod, she relaxes back in the leather seat behind her desk.

"Mr. Dahl is on an extended business trip and cannot meet you. However, he wants the position filled before he returns next week. My team and I have a few other candidates to interview before I make the final decision. Either way, we will be in touch. Thank you for meeting with us, Wren. My administrative assistant will see you to the elevators. Good day."

Tag

"Good morning, Mr. Dahl."

"Hello, Mr. Dahl, sir."

I nod brusquely in response to the greetings from staff as I stride through The Larson Tower lobby towards the executive floor elevator.

Even though it's been weeks since the charity gala, I'm still on edge. No matter how much I searched the terrace, ballroom, hell, even the entire hotel, I couldn't find the she-wolf with the unique scent of my fated mate. Talk about frustration.

But I set the pursuit aside because of a business trip the next day. Not able to cancel it, I had no other choice but to spend the past three weeks in our Charleston, Atlanta, New Orleans, and Houston offices.

At least once every other quarter, I show up unannounced. No better way to gauge productivity and to check on staff behavior than to catch them unaware. Rarely do I find problems requiring reprimand since our leadership team does an excellent job of running their offices.

Most of the team comprises members of the Miami Wolves Pack. Their loyalty and respect keep them on the straight and narrow. Naturally, their share in the profits as pack members serve as serious encouragement. The human team members do not disappoint—most of the time.

It was a successful trip. But I'm glad to be back at headquarters.

I check the time on my watch. Before the weekly staff meeting at nine, the Head of Human Resources—a she-wolf—has my new social assistant scheduled to arrive at my offices. I reviewed her application—along with the other top five candidates—and agree on paper she's the best choice. I added a sixty-day trial period clause in her contract just in case. She doesn't appear Katrina-like. But who knows?

My mobile chimes with an incoming text message. I take it out of the breast pocket of my bespoke three-piece suit. I smirk at the mobile screen. Viggo invites me to a party for a popular human female singer at Club Hati— one of Larson Enterprises' venues in his portfolio. He chose the name as a nod to Norse mythology. The wolf Hati chases the moon, across the night sky. His counterpart the wolf Sköll chases the sun during the day. They do so until the time of Ragnarök when they will swallow the heavenly bodies. The club caters to wolf shifters and humans.

I shrug. Why not? I could use a distraction after these past few weeks. My wolf and I need more sexual release than my hand allows, but nothing more than a one-nighter. At this point in my life, I don't want a relationship and none of the drama that comes along with one.

And that includes pushing aside the dull ache for my fated mate's touch. It's best I can't find the elusive she-wolf. Undoubtedly, I *can* find a nice morsel to feast upon at the party and get my mind off a fated mate. My cock twitches at the thought as I reply to Viggo's text.

Punching in the code for the private elevator, I adjust the burgeoning erection then step inside. The elevator will automatically go to the executive floor since it's the only stop besides the lobby. As the doors close, a female's manicured fingers—one with an engagement ring—slip between the bit of space. I frown. Only the C-suite uses this elevator. The rest of the staff take the general elevators. Who the hell is this?

Then it hits me dead on this time.

The tantalizing aroma of cinnamon sugar caramel apples. The scent of my fated mate—the only she-wolf destined for me.

Forget burgeoning. My cock punches the front of my trousers instantly. A growl rumbles in my chest. My wolf throws his massive brown head back and issues a feral, lust-filled howl. My nostrils flare as I inhale deeply.

Emerald green eyes flash as they narrow on the slit between the elevator doors.

Who *are* you?

The doors slide open.

A petite human female in a body skimming green dress that stops at the midpoint of her shapely calves ending in fuck-me stilettos with a sexy touch of toe cleavage enters. The fit of the dress accentuates her mouthwatering tits and luscious curves. Lustrous mahogany brown hair ripples down her back. Soulful mink brown eyes widen as her pouty lips form a perfect O. A rose flush licks at her exposed collarbone, up her throat, and to her cheeks. The first taste of her arousal teases me, increasing the saliva pooling in my hungry mouth.

The doors slide close.

 *ren*

"Whoa, Wren! Look at you. Your new boss better watch out or he just may fall in love with you at first sight regardless of the no employer-employee relationships stipulation!"

I giggle at Maya's compliment, then glance down at the new outfit for my first day at Larson Enterprises.

The goal isn't to make Mr. Dahl fall for me. Rather, I want to combine the style of a socialite with my budding confidence.

The jewel green midi dress flatters my BBW figure. The interlocking twist drape bodice, darted seams, and fitted skirt highlight my curves just enough without going beyond professional. Flesh-tone slingbacks lengthen my legs and give my generous butt a nice lift. A hunter green top-handle bag finishes the look.

"It's not too much, is it?" I ask as I nibble my lower lip, now concerned. "I don't want to give off the wrong impression. Maybe I should wear the—"

"Oh no, you won't. This is perfect. You're not going to work at a corporate law office. The company is in the hospitality industry—clubs, hotels, restaurants. Plus, you're his *social* assistant, not his accountant."

Maya picks up my handbag and ushers me out of the dressing room towards the front door of my condo. I laugh and take the bag, then loop my arm through hers. We part in the garage. She hugs me and tells me good luck. I grin and thank her.

The drive to The Larson Tower takes no time. I bop to the music from my encouragement playlist to pump me up. Beyoncé's "Run The World (Girls)" blasts from the surround sound. My left foot taps to the beat. Yes!

I don't even care when a guy in a sleek sports car frowns at me. Instead, I wave and zip ahead when the traffic light changes. My confidence rises with the speedometer—although I stay within the posted limit. Let's not go crazy, now!

In the lobby, I present my employee badge to the security guards behind their station, then follow where a guard points to the elevators. As I approach one, the doors begin to shut. Not wanting to risk a late arrival to meet Mr. Dahl, I rush forward and slip my hand in the gap. Relieved, I step inside.

I freeze.

The provocative scent of vetiver seamlessly blended with citrus, rich spices, and fresh woods fills my nose as the cologne sensuously molds around my body. Nipples tighten, that sensitive nubbin at the apex of my thighs pulses as my gaze settles on an impeccably dressed man. He's so tall, my eyes only reach his powerful chest. They scan up his muscular body to broad shoulders and to a face kissed by Aphrodite herself.

A dimpled chin with a dusting of sable brown stubble leads to a kissable mouth. The nostrils of his nose flare. My breath hitches as his flashing green eyes narrow on me. The intensity of his stare heats my cheeks.

Before me stands Tag Dahl—the most gorgeous man I have ever seen. The photos online fail to capture his masculine beauty. And his charismatic pull.

The doors close behind me.

I gasp at the sound of a low growl. If a man wasn't standing there, I would bet a wild wolf lurked within the elevator shaft. A shiver snakes down my spine, and I don't think it's from fear.

"Who *are* you?"

His gruff, smokey voice skitters over my skin like a lover's teasing caress. The promise of the carnal pleasure to come.

My mouth opens to respond. But words can't form. I blink and breathe through my open mouth. Before my next attempt, I cough to clear my throat. Like steel to a magnet, our eyes find one another again. A yearning grows deep within me. My lips part.

The lights flicker.

With a frown, I lift my gaze to the ceiling.

The elevator jounces.

It drops a few feet.

The lights flick off.

Pitch black.

Instead of words, a scream rips past my lips as I tumble against Mr. Dahl. Strong hands hold me close to his firm chest. The scent of his cologne makes me dizzy with need. I bite back another cry mixed with an unexpected lusty moan.

"I've got you," he growls, a deep rumble in his chest.

There's that wolf again. Now, I know the sound emanates from him and isn't a figment of my imagination.

Just like your father. You have the most vivid imagination!

A nervous giggle bubbles up as my mind replays a memory of Uncle George complaining about my creativity. He found my hidden stash of drawing pads, where I sketched the fantastical creatures I read about in my favorite story books. Witches, wolves, trolls, fairies, elves, and more filled the pages. They were my escape from my depressing reality.

But it's my fear of tight places that strikes panic in me. If Wretched Gretchen felt I misbehaved, she locked me in a dark closet for hours. Her threat to throw away my photo albums kept me from telling Uncle George. I knew he wouldn't care since he wanted me to forget my parents all together.

Now, I cling to Mr. Dahl. Fingers scrunch his soft wool suit jacket. My heart thuds as I bury my face in his chest. Hysteria grips me.

"It's all right. The elevator stopping will alert the building maintenance and the security staff," Mr. Dahl says. His warm breath blows across the crown of my head as he curls his enormous body over me. "I'm going to let go of you with one hand so I can hit the intercom button. Do you understand?"

My fingers grip tighter. A sob escapes.

A large palm strokes my back as a rumble vibrates beneath my cheek. I feel it throughout my body—a calming rhythm.

"Mr. Dahl, sir! Are you all right?"

A disembodied voice breaks the moment.

He stiffens. The strokes and the rumble cease.

I whimper.

His hand and the vibrations resume as he responds.

"Yes. What the hell happened?!"

Although he's soothing me, I sense his anger and frustration. I try my best to calm down. I don't want to make the situation worse. God forbid we're stuck here for more than a few minutes. I shudder. He growls.

"Tell me something. Now!"

"Yes, sir, Mr. Dahl. There's no issue on the security end. The Head of Building Maintenance is checking his system as we speak, sir. Please give us a moment. We will respond as soon as possible."

Another displeased growl follows.

"Fine. Tell my administrative assistant I'm stuck in the elevator. I also have a Ms. Wren Byrd due in my office. If she's checked in, tell her, too. Otherwise, have Beth contact her."

"Yes, sir, Mr. Dahl. Right away, sir!"

I lift my cheek from his chest to glance up at him, then remember he won't be able to see my face. I'm nervous to tell him I'm Wren Byrd since he bit the head off the security guard. Geez.

"Um… Mr. Dahl?"

"Are you all right? It won't be long. I know you're frightened. Just try to relax. I'll keep you safe. As you heard, they're working on the situation."

He tightens his grip on my waist with one arm and strokes my back with the other hand.

It feels so good to be held lovingly. I haven't felt such warm affection since my parents. Tears burn my eyes. But I hold them back. I must remain focused.

"I understand, sir."

I pause when a ripple runs through him. A moan threatens to slip out of my mouth. I swallow it back down with a shake of my head.

So inappropriate, Wren! I chide myself.

But I can't help the sensations flowing through me. I close my eyes, take a deep cleansing breath, and try again with more conviction.

"Mr. Dahl, sir, I'm Wren Byrd."

He sucks in a breath. His body turns rigid. The moment he steps away from me, the loss of his heat chills my soul. I cry out.

"I—I… This comes as a surprise. Excuse my inappropriate behavior. It didn't occur to me you are my new social assistant."

Each word spoken drives a nail into my heart.

My arms wrap around my torso in a protective manner. The darkness and closeness of the stuck elevator threaten to overwhelm me. His loss makes it a thousand times worse. I regret admitting my identity, dammit!

"Mr. Dahl, sir," I try again, speaking in the direction he withdrew. "I appreciate your… behavior. I must admit, it calmed my nerves. You see, I'm afraid of close quarters and the dark makes it unbearable."

A rumbling comes from his corner.

My knees weaken in relief.

I reach for the wall as they buckle.

But before I hit the floor, strong arms embrace me. His heat and intoxicating cologne engulf me. I sag against him once again. Tears pool in my eyes, squeezed shut.

"Thank you," I sigh as my arms wrap around his waist. Despite the facts he's my new boss and we have a non-fraternization clause, I hold Tag Dahl with all of my might.

Tag

. . .

MY ENHANCED VISION allows me to see Wren Byrd clearly in the elevator's darkness. Her eyes set in a face etched with fright, stare pleadingly in my direction. She can't see me but senses my presence. My wolf claws beneath my skin. He wants to break free and comfort what he considers his fated mate. It takes more effort than I expected, but I tamp him down. He returns to the fringes of my being with a disgruntled howl.

I recall the movie "The Gods Must Be Crazy" and how a foreign object causes such chaos in a peaceful, controlled environment. Instead of a Coca-Cola bottle dropping from the sky to disturb the people, Wren Byrd—my human social assistant—lands in my arms. She bears the unique scent of my fated mate. The only one for me. And she's a *human* female. Not a she-wolf. And she's engaged.

No. Fucking. Way.

I'd fall over laughing hysterically if I thought this was some sort of dumb prank Viggo—the jokester of our group—pulled on me. Unfortunately, it's all too real.

Her delicious scent fills my nostrils as I hold her close. The instinctive urge to comfort her causes a soothing rumble to emanate from my chest. My feral wolf howls, disturbed by our fated mate's distress. We want to console her in more ways than rumbles and back strokes.

My aching cock wants to drive into her warm, wet pussy made only for me over and over and over again. Until she writhes beneath me, screaming my name in carnal bliss, not in abject fear. Then expand my knot to seal us together as my seed floods her womb, placing my pup in her belly.

Mine!

Fuck. Me.

But I cannot allow this to happen.

For one, I'm not interested in a relationship beyond satisfying my sexual needs. I'm too busy for it and don't want the drama. So, it's good she's engaged.

Two, she's a human. No male wolf shifter in our pack has turned a human into a she-wolf in for-fucking-ever. It's dangerous and can cause her death. Not something to do on a whim driven by the attraction to a fated mate.

Three—and above all—Wren Byrd is an employee of Larson Enterprises, Inc., my social assistant, my subordinate. We have a non-fraternization clause in her contract. I cannot get involved with her. No way.

This whole situation is screwed.

"Mr. Dahl, sir?"

"Yes?! What's the status?" I snap as my barely contained frustration and anger threaten to overflow. As it stands, my control hangs on by one wolf whisker. And damn if it's not about to fray as her sweet scent entices me.

"Yes, sir. Maintenance confirmed there's a fault in the machine room. He estimates the repair's completion in... um... twenty minutes. He apologizes for the inconvenience, sir."

I growl, knowing the security guard will sense my

displeasure since he's a member of our pack. My keen wolf hearing picks up his thick swallow.

"Do all of you realize this could have been a major disaster?! I want a full report on my desk in thirty minutes, including the status of all elevators, their repair and inspection histories, warranties, etc. Do you understand?"

"Y—Yes, bet—ah, Mr. Dahl. sir."

I narrow my eyes as I glare at the intercom for his almost slip-up in referring to me as our pack beta. Not good. At. All. A human would wonder what he means. And I have one trembling in my arms as we speak.

"Ms. Wren Byrd is here with me. Be mindful of your choice in words. Also, no need to inform her of my situation."

Another stuttered acknowledgment, and the intercom falls silent.

My mind returns to the dilemma.

I can't have Wren Byrd as my fated mate.

Can I have her as my social assistant and not issue the claiming bite?

My wolf stares with flashing emerald green eyes as the serum to initiate her transformation into a she-wolf drips from his exposed fangs.

Talk about pure havoc wreaking my structured life and driving my wolf feral. This curvaceous human female's been in my life for less than ten minutes and shit's already turned upside down.

As though sensing the inner conflict roiling within me, Wren Byrd whimpers. Her fingers clutch at my back. The softness of her lush body molds to the hard planes of mine calling to my cock like a Siren.

My wolf howls demandingly.

I stiffen.

Fuck. Me. Or. What.

CHAPTER 5

ag

"MR. DAHL, SIR?"

Fortunately, the security guard interrupts my thoughts. I use his call as an excuse to gently extricate myself from Wren Byrd. Her soft gasp nudges the heart I'm trying to harden. My wolf paces on the fringes, eyeing me. I ignore all of it and respond.

"How's the progress?" I bark into the intercom speaker.

An audible gulp answers my question.

"Do not tell me there is no change in the status. Do not disappoint me."

A different voice responds.

"Excuse me, Mr. Dahl. We don't have the part required

for the repair. The elevator company rep will arrive with it in thirty minutes based on traffic—"

I shout.

Wren wails.

Silence on the other end.

I ream the Head of Maintenance out for not having the proper supplies on hand. The situation could be a lot more critical as in a pregnant female on board or a medical emergency. I demand a full accounting of the elevator systems by the end of the day. He apologizes profusely and assures me they will fix the problem as soon as the rep arrives. I end the communication and pivot to check on Wren Byrd.

My heart clenches at the sight of her huddled in the corner. Eyes closed. Knees bent with her arms wrapped around them. She rocks back and forth. Her lips move. Even with my keen hearing, the words are too low to decipher.

I rush over and crouch in front of her. Hands on her shoulders, I stop her movement.

"Ms. Byrd, I know this must be an unimaginable horror for you. However, as you heard, the crew expects to get us out of here soon. Until then, rest assured, I will allow nothing to happen to you. We will get through this situation together. Do you understand?"

She mumbles incoherently as tears stream down her pale cheeks.

My protective instinct kicks in. I drop to the floor. One arm wraps around her shoulders to angle her body into mine, while the other arm encircles her and clasps my opposite hand. She melts against me with the top of her head beneath my chin and her knees pressed to my chest, curled into a ball. I can't help but to notice she fits with me perfectly.

My nose burrows in her hair. A deep inhalation suffuses every cell in my body with her unique cinnamon sugar caramel apples scent. One by one, the cells spark, crackling with electricity. The sensation spreads from my heart out through each limb. It ignites my brain like a headstart jolt from a jumper cable.

Engaged or not, Wren Byrd is my fated mate.

Whether or not I want her.

The realization unsettles me.

My wolf? He struts, tail high.

I ignore his triumphant parade.

The rest of the time, I hold Wren close. The rumble emanating from deep within my chest soothes her. By the time the lights flicker on and the elevator ascends, she's quiet with her eyes shut. I cradle her in my arms and rise.

We emerge onto the executive floor to find half a dozen people gathered at the elevator doors, including the staff nurse. Ignoring the others clamoring, I tell her to follow me to my office suite. Wren's care takes priority above all else.

I lay her on the sofa in the sitting area of my office and stand.

Her eyelids flutter but don't open. She mumbles again as she reaches for me.

As I stare down at her, I have to admit I miss the warmth of her body. My arms feel empty without her in them. My fingers flex with the urge to grab her close.

A polite cough reminds me of the staff nurse and Beth's presence. I nod and stride to the built-in beverage center. Removing two bottles of water, I return to the sofa and place one on the coffee table.

Wren's eyes open as the staff nurse speaks to her gently. But instead of looking at her, they scan the room until they find mine. Her sad mink brown orbs tug at my heart. I rub the ache in my chest.

In my periphery, Beth's eyebrows raise to her hairline in surprise. The staff nurse glances at me over her shoulder, hand suspended with a moist cloth.

It's then I notice the rumble started again.

As mated she-wolves, they recognize the sound of a male wolf shifter soothing his mate.

Fuck!

They'll suspect something between Wren and me. I cannot have staff or pack members aware of this unresolved set of circumstances. From a company standpoint, Wren is my subordinate. As for the pack, they'll question a human female being turned. And as the Alpha, Jagger would need to know first.

Beyond all that lies the problem of me being undecided. For once in my well-thought-out life, I have no idea what to do. It's not a simple solution.

The magnetism to a fated mate proves irresistible, especially for the male wolf shifter. The inherent urge to care for, protect, and to breed the female is instant and increases over time. If the mate bond cannot complete, the male suffers from madness as he loses control of his wolf. Roles reverse and the wolf becomes the dominate. No pack allows a rampant wolf. They kill it. And that damn sure is not a part of my life plan.

Plus, I can't harm Wren. She's practically comatose from getting stuck in the elevator. Not that I don't empathize with her. But the transition from human to wolf takes a toll on the body and adjusting to being a wolf shifter impacts the psyche. She's a fragile human and may not survive the claiming bite or handle the mental aspect of it all.

And she's engaged to another male.

What a clusterfuck.

So, I back away from the sofa, where Wren stares beseechingly at me. She doesn't understand the reason for the attraction she feels for me but knows she needs it. She continues to seek my comfort without looking at Beth or the staff nurse.

Again, my heart clenches. But I fight the urge and maintain a stoic expression. I refuse to add to the potential gossip.

Behind me, my office door bursts open.

"Tag, damn. How are you and Ms. Byrd?" Jagger asks as he storms inside. His ice blue eyes survey the scene, then focus on me. A slight frown draws his white blonde eyebrows together. Imperceptibly, he sniffs the air. The frown deepens. He opens his mouth to speak. But I cut him off.

"Beth, get Ms. Byrd whatever she needs. She will remain on the sofa until I return momentarily," I say, then nod at Jagger to follow me before I march from my office and shut the door. "Let's talk in your office."

He nods.

We enter his office suite next to mine. He tells his administrative assistant Ginny to hold his calls as we pass his reception area, where she sits at her desk. I shut his office door while he strides to the desk. He presses the privacy button to darken the glass walls. I slump on a sofa. My hands drag down my face with a growl.

"Okay, what the hell is going on? Why do I sense a bond between you and Ms. Byrd? Hell, I even sense her as I do members of our pack. Talk to me, Tag."

He lowers his massive frame onto the chair opposite me. Keen eyes focus on my face.

As the Alpha, Jagger has a connection to each member of the Miami Wolves Pack. He can sense our emotional states and detect danger to us. Similar to the bond shared between mates. It's his internal radar.

And right now, I wish he didn't have it. I'm no closer to knowing what to do and not ready to discuss it. However, he is my Alpha. I must heed his command, especially as his beta and his right hand. It is the order of the pack.

I scrub my face again as I shake my head and blow a breath.

"Wren Byrd is my new social assistant. *Human* social assistant."

I pause to roll my eyes to the ceiling as though the answer lies above. Yeah, well, I've already established the gods must be crazy. So, I doubt I'll get any sane guidance from them. At least, none that I want since they made the fated mate pairing to begin with. Annoyed, my mouth twists to the side.

"There's more to it than that, Tag. Spill it."

Right. It certainly is a lot more.

"Wren Byrd is my fated mate. A human female. Not a she-wolf. And she's engaged."

I drop the bombshell and sit back as it detonates in the room.

Jagger's mouth drops open.

Mine twists.

"Are you absolutely certain?"

"Cinnamon sugar caramel apples."

He frowns.

I lean forward with my elbows on my knees and steeple my fingers.

"The aroma of my first breath when I was born—cinnamon sugar caramel apples. Wren Byrd bears that unique scent. Funny enough, I first detected it the night of the charity gala a few weeks ago. Out on the rooftop terrace. I searched but couldn't find her anywhere. Today, she steps onto the executive elevator—still not sure why security directed her to it—and her scent overpowered me. My wolf went feral."

I sit back and growl in frustration.

"So, yeah, I'm absolutely certain she's my fated mate. However, I have no clue what to do about it."

Jagger stares at me for what seems like an hour, but really is only a minute. He stands and paces the floor. His hands slip into the trouser pockets of his suit. The same height as me, his long legs cross from one end to the other quickly. He stops and focuses on me.

"An engaged human female. Damn, that's messy bro. If the memory of our pack history serves me correctly, it's been at least thirty years since a transition took place. It was before we were even born. But it stands out sadly."

He returns to the chair and leans forward, eyes intense.

My gut churns. I already know it's not something I want to hear. At. All. I close my eyes a moment, then reopen them, determined to face reality no matter what.

"The male wolf shifter fell in love with a human female. He explained his true nature to her. She accepted him and wanted to be one with him in all ways. He asked my father as the Alpha for permission to grant her the gift. He agreed based on past experiences.

"Prior to them, others were successful, or, for whatever odd reason, the transition didn't take fully. Those partial transitions resulted in the females not being able to shift, but they gained the traits to live longer and better health."

He pauses.

I lean forward, needing to know the outcome of the last pair.

Jagger nods and continues.

"Sadly, the human female died. She never recovered from the claiming bite. Her agony drove the male mad since he blamed himself. When she passed away, he went into the Everglades and never returned. My father and several males searched for him. They only found his remains left by a panther."

I recoil.

Just as I thought. I can't risk Wren's life. She may be my fated mate and the attraction is powerful. But I will not subject her to agony. It was bad enough to watch her tremble in the elevator and to lie comatose on the sofa. Not happening. No. I resign myself to end Wren's contract and to avoid any contact with her. It's for the best.

"Hold on, Tag."

Jagger's voice pulls me back to the room.

"An important difference is key," he starts and waits for me to look at him. I face him. "Remember, I said he fell in love with her. They and the partial transition pairs were not fated mates. The successful ones were."

My eyes bug. No way!

He nods.

"You confirmed Wren is your fated mate by her unique scent. The chances of her transition being positive are high. You'll have more of a hard time getting rid of the fiancé and explaining your true nature to her, so she accepts you. Then she would have to give you permission to bestow the gift. It is her decision to become a she-wolf. I will not allow you or anyone else to force a human female or a she-wolf to complete a mate bond. And if she doesn't agree, we can't have a human know of our existence. The risk is too great. So be sure you've gotten her to fall for you completely before telling her what we are. Are you clear?"

"Yes, Alpha."

Not only are the gods crazy, I must be too.

Wren's contract has the sixty-day trial period clause in it. I have two months to figure out what the hell to do.

CHAPTER 6

ren

"Oh, honey! I'm so sorry! What happens now?"

Maya sits back from hugging me.

I still can't believe that whole elevator fiasco. One minute, I'm all excited about my first day at work. The next I'm face-to-face with my new boss, struck dumb by his sexiness before the elevator falls apart! Then I'm thrown into his strapping arms, where I proceed to lose my damn mind. And not just from claustrophobia but from his alluring masculinity.

Even now, hours later, my nipples pebble. They're so sensitive the silk bra makes them ache. I press my thighs together to soothe the needy warmth pooling in my core just at the thought of Tag Dahl. The beast of a man who yells at others. Yet he's a giant teddy bear holding me close.

I wrap my own arms around myself in a sorry attempt to mimic his sweet embrace. And the way his sizable hands caressed my back. Oh, and I can't forget the rumble in his massive chest. The vibrations did all sorts of things to my lady bits. My goodness!

But I would have appreciated it more had I not panicked. Thanks, Wretched Gretchen...

Genuine fear gripped me. But his presence eased the terror. Unfortunately, the amount of time we spent in the elevator finished me off. I couldn't function despite his attempts to calm me. I retreated to the depths of my being, as I did years ago. My safe space welcomed me like an old friend.

I didn't rouse from it until the staff nurse spoke to me in soothing tones. My only waking thought was to find Tag Dahl. When our eyes connected, I felt instant relief. His mere presence touched me deep inside. The rumble resonated within. But when he left abruptly, my heart sank.

I watched him leave the office. When the door closed behind him, I turned my head and closed my eyes. A sense of loss washed over me. With him gone, I returned to my safe space.

The staff nurse declared I was in shock and needed to rest. She placed pillows beneath my legs and a cashmere throw over me. His administrative assistant handed a bottle of water to me and asked if I needed anything else.

I shook my head and thanked them.

They told me to stay put until Mr. Dahl returned. I murmured my assent while inwardly I prayed he wouldn't be long. I must have dozed off because I awoke to him calling my name. My eyes fluttered open.

"Wren, how do you feel?"

His emerald green eyes appear darker, more like jade as he stares at me. Concern fills them as he studies my face intently.

I have the urge to cup his cheek. My eyes lower to his lips. The urge to nibble on the plump lower one makes me draw my own into my mouth. I drop my gaze. A growl snaps it to his face.

A flash of something crosses it before he turns away and strides to his desk. His muscular legs make quick work of the distance. But it's too far for me.

I sit up and swing my feet to the floor. Our eyes meet again when he folds his body into the leather chair behind his desk. A frisson runs through me. I tremble and wrap my arms around my torso.

With grace unexpected of a man his size, he leaps to his feet and hastens back to me. He crouches and removes my slingbacks. His touch causes sparks to skitter across my skin. His fingers pause, then he places my legs on the pillows. The throw covers me.

"Do not move," he says in a thick, rough voice. "The staff nurse says you are in shock. Be still."

His commanding tone takes me by surprise. I gasp. His eyes snap to mine. If I'm not mistaken, a carnal hunger lurks in their depths. But he blinks, and the moment passes. Perhaps I was mistaken. I shake my head and lean against the pillow.

"I—I just wanted to answer your question, Mr. Dahl, sir," I

stammer as I watch him from beneath the thick fringe of my eyelashes. For some reason, I want to show him I'm not challenging him in any way—merely responding.

He grunts a nod.

I take it as permission to continue.

"Well, I'm a bit embarrassed by—"

"No. Do not feel that way, Wren."

I swallow as that tone tingles over my body.

"Go on."

I blink and nod.

"It's claustrophobia. So, thank you for keeping me calm. Usually, elevators don't bother me so much. I recognize the doors will open soon, and I can get off. This time... Well... You know," I end on a shudder and pull the throw tighter around me.

The rumble fills the space between us.

My head jerks in his direction.

"What is that sound you make?"

I bite my lip when his cheeks flush. The sound stops. I miss it immediately and wish I hadn't said a word about it. Big mouth, Wren!

He clears his throat and buttons his suit jacket. I admire the way it drapes over his body, so well tailored to enhance his fit form. He coughs politely, and I blush at being caught staring at his crotch. I can't help it being at eye level or noticing his broad length along a thigh. Holy moly.

My eyes track up his body to his handsome face. Another flash crosses it.

"I have meetings to attend outside of the office for the rest of the morning. You stay here until you feel better. Then go home.

Beth will arrange a car for you. If you're up to it, come in tomorrow morning at nine. Otherwise, inform her you're unable to make it. No rush. I want you at your best, Wren."

Why did my mind hear, I want you flipped over on the sofa, knees wide, back arched, pussy bare and dripping???

I press my thighs together, thankful the throw hides the movement. Talk about embarrassing...

Get a damn grip, Wren Byrd! I'm no virgin. But such lustful thoughts never entered my mind before. And Jonathan certainly doesn't evoke them. He's handsome to thrill me. But in the bedroom? It's pretty cut and dry. No steam and definitely no spice.

But my new boss? That's a whole other naughty story.

"Yes, Mr. Dahl, sir. I appreciate your understanding since this is my first day, and it didn't go quite as planned. However, I expect to make it in tomorrow. I hope you have productive meetings."

He watches me for a moment, then nods and strides from the office.

As though he took the air from my lungs, I gasp and flop back on the sofa.

My focus returns to Maya to answer her question.

"Now, I go in tomorrow and not make a fool of myself," I say, then giggle. "I wish I could take the stairs!"

Maya falls back against the sofa and laughs. I join in until a stitch forms in my side. She wipes the tears from her eyes as she sits up.

"Chica! You crack me up. What a way to pivot from an unpleasant situation. Good for you!"

I grin and shake my head.

"Oh, Maya, I have a confession."

Her eyes widen as her eyebrows rise.

I bow my head and mumble.

"Speak up, Wren! You have me on pins and needles here."

"I'm attracted to Tag Dahl."

She gasps and covers her mouth with both hands.

"I know. I know. He's my boss. The non-fraternization clause. Manager and subordinate. Blah, blah blah. I'm a mess and can't help it!"

I admit to my erotic fantasies. Maya sympathizes.

"Okay, I get falling for that sexy as sin hottie. But what about Jonathan? What have you decided?"

Ah, yes, my not-so-faithful fiancé.

After the charity gala, he sort of called me, not the next day as he said he would do. Rather, a few days later, he sent a text message asserting he was busy. Then he had a business trip he extended to a Guys' Getaway. He returned yesterday. I haven't heard from him other than brief conversations or texts.

Not that I mind.

It gave me time to realize we're not right for one another. I choose to value myself more than being happy a hot guy wants me as his wife. Who knows if that was the first time he cheated on me? And maybe with others besides his sassy and slim neighbor, for all I know. I'd rather be alone than with a man who doesn't respect me.

Now, Uncle George, on the other hand, will have a conniption when I tell him my decision. Undoubtedly, he'll attempt to berate me and to make me change my mind. However, I'll stand firm. Well, at least try to ignore whatever hurtful things he may say. I won't marry Jonathan, regardless.

"Hi, honey, I'm home!"

I sit up with a gasp.

God, please let this be my vivid imagination. Please!

As though I conjured him up, Jonathan struts into the living room from the entry foyer. His turquoise blue eyes glitter at the running joke of his announcement when he arrives at my condo. Right now, I don't giggle. Instead, I fight to keep my eyes from rolling heavenward. Thanks for nothing.

Maya folds her arms over her chest. She pins him with a fierce glare. Topaz eyes flash.

"*Bueno, habla del diablo*," she mutters under her breath with a toss of her waist-long hair. "I'll stay, if you want me to."

I give a slight shake of my head.

"*Hola*, Maya, lovely to see you as always," Jonathan smirks. They have an open dislike for one another. Who could blame Maya?

The more I look at him now, the more I see the jerk she always said he was. I sigh at the time wasted.

"*Adiós, tramposo*," she responds, then turns and hugs me. "Call me later."

I nod and watch her leave.

Jonathan glares after her. Once she's out the door, he huffs.

"What the hell? A tramp? I'm far from a bum!"

I stifle a giggle. Better he thinks she called him a tramp and not a cheater—the actual translation.

"You need better friends than her, Wren. How many times do I have to tell you no one makes friends with the help, including personal trainers. Your uncle and aunt agree with me."

Anger boils up from my core like a dormant volcano spewing lava to the sky. I rise from the sofa. My fists bunch at my sides. I narrow a scorching glare at him. Through clenched teeth, I snarl.

"How. *Dare*. You."

Jonathan's head jerks back so fast he may suffer whiplash. His mouth gapes, stunned by my ferociousness. Eyes skitter across my face.

"Maya is far from the help! She is my best friend. If your head wasn't so far up your ass, you would pay attention to me and know I told you she comes from a wealthy Venezuelan family, as in petroleum. And even if she didn't, she's still my. Best. Friend!"

His mouth gapes like a fish out of water. Shock registers in his eyes. Along with dollar, no bolívar signs. What an absolute jerk!

"You know what, Jonathan? I'm glad you're here. It saves me from having to make a phone call."

He shakes his head to clear it and cocks it questioningly.

I remove the engagement ring from my finger.

His eyes bulge as I jam it into his chest.

"I will not marry you. It's over."

Stunned, he stares at me. When he recovers, he shakes his head.

"All because I said you need better friends? For real, Wren? Give me a break. Now, cut it out and put your ring back on."

He reaches for my hand.

I tuck both under my crossed arms.

"No. And if you believe the only reason is your rudeness to Maya, you are beyond clueless, Jonathan," I say with narrowed eyes. My heart races, but I refuse to back down. "You cheated on me with your neighbor, and who knows who else? You tell me I don't satisfy you—"

"Now, hold on, Wren. I never said that—"

I hold up my hand, palm out.

"You don't have to. Your body language speaks volumes. A few pokes, and you roll off and take a shower. Am I that gross to you?" I shake my head. "You know what? Don't answer that. Whatever you say is irrelevant. Just go, Jonathan. We're done. I am done with you."

I storm past him. He grabs my arm. But I snatch it from his grasp and continue to the entry foyer. I ignore his calls to stop. As I fling the door open, I turn and point at him.

"You, out. Now!"

"Come on, Wren. You can't be serious. How about we compromise? I'll give you some time to get yourself together. When you're ready, I'll be waiting. Deal?"

He approaches me with his hand outstretched for a shake.

I stare at it like a poisonous snake set to strike the death blow.

"No. No deal, Jonathan. Despite what you may think, I never agreed to marry you because of what my uncle intends for my betrothed. I fell in love with you. And what good did it do me, huh? A *tramposo*! That's what I got. No, thank you. Now, go, Jonathan."

The veil falls from his countenance. A nasty sneer appears as he narrows his eyes and curls his lip. Nostrils flare.

The vehemence makes me step back. I clutch the door, pulling it closer to me like a shield. What the hell?

"You know what, Wren? I don't have to take your bullshit. You're lucky to have someone like me even bother with someone like you—a fat, frigid, pathetic girl. But I tell you this much. Your uncle will not allow you to bail on this *marriage*. It's a deal you will commit to whether or not you want it. So, get over yourself. I'll see you around, Wren."

Jonathan drops the engagement ring on the table and stalks past me. He casts another disgusted glare over his shoulder as he presses the elevator call button.

Heart racing and tears in my eyes, I slam the door.

"YES, Mr. Dahl, Sir. I will get those notes for you right away."

I watch Wren's generous hips sway in a form-fitting skirt as she sashays to the conference table. She bends over it, reaching for the file folder on the opposite side. An arm extends across the surface. The other grips the edge. Her back arches and lifts that mouth-watering round ass in the air. It's like a red flag before a bull. Or, in my case, a delicious morsel dangled in front of a hungry wolf.

A growl emanates from deep within my chest.

She shudders and tosses her long mane of glossy mahogany brown hair over her shoulder. Wide eyes peek at me. Gold glints in their mink brown depths. She wiggles her hips.

My tongue lolls.

My cock thickens.

It weeps a tear of pre-cum.

Slowly, she rises.

"Do. Not. Move."

I growl and leap to my feet. Like the famished apex predator I am, I stalk my prey. "Stretch out across the table. Palms flat. Head down. Ass up."

Her soft mewl sends my wolf baying.

I tower over her. Hands grip her hips. A foot kicks hers further apart. As wide as the tight skirt allows. My enhanced hearing picks up the increase in her heart rate. My nose detects her musky arousal. She moans.

A claw extends.

The sharp tip cuts her silk blouse from the collar and along her spine. The soft fabric slips down her sides to pool on the table. A flick of my wrist, and the bra fasteners pop. The black lace joins the silk. I trail the claw further down her spine. Goosebumps follow in its wake.

She shivers. And not from the cold. A lusty moan pours from her slack mouth. Her hips roll.

I smirk.

My hand brushes the voluptuous curve of her ass. I swing my arm back. My palm lands with a satisfying THWACK on one large globe. The soft flesh jiggles beneath my hand. The sensation zips up my arm and down to my erect cock. It twitches, eager to get in on the action.

My wolf scratches to be free. To take what he knows is ours to have.

I agree.

My arm rises and spanks the other ass cheek.

This time, Wren cries out. She dances on her tiptoes. She mewls when I squeeze her hip.

"Do. Not. Move."

I growl in her ear. My warm breath tickles the delicate shell. I trace it with the tip of my tongue. She starts to shiver, then catches herself. She moans. Pressed against her, I angle my pelvis for my cock to rest at the crack of her ass. Her whimper makes it thump in my trousers.

"If you want this, Red, you better obey."

Yeah, she's the innocent little girl to my beast of a wolf. And I will corrupt her in every imaginable way. Just how I know she wants it. Nice and filthy. Isn't that what all good little girls really want?

I smirk and stand.

The skirt proves no match to my capable hands. It rips in two. Only three strings circle her hips and slip between her ass cheeks. I pluck the G-string from her body, sniff it deeply, and place it in my pocket. My eyes lift to find her peeking at me, crimson colors her cheeks. I curl my lip and growl. She closes her eyes and shudders with a soft cry.

I chuckle wickedly.

My palm beats a quick staccato on her ass. Left, right, underside, right, left, underside. Again, and again. She yelps and pants. The sweet ambrosia of her arousal fills the air. I'm dizzy from it. Three fingers trace her puffy lower lips, slick with her juices.

A desperate moan seeps from her mouth. She shifts her pelvis to catch my fingers on her engorged clit. Her moan turns into a strangled cry when I spank her pussy with those same fingers.

"Oh! Oh! Oh! Oh!"

"Did I not command you to remain still, naughty girl?" I growl in her ear. "Now, you will not cum on my cock. But *I* will cum. Down. Your. Throat."

She whimpers as I spin her around. I tear the remnants of her blouse and bra from her body. Ripe tits bounce freely. Their thick nipples tighten, begging to be suckled. With a growl, I oblige them.

My mouth latches on to one plump tip. It hardens further as my tongue circles around it. I nibble on the succulent morsel, groaning. Fingers tweak the other nipple, keeping it primed for me. My sizable hands easily toy with the hefty weight of her double Ds. I make a savory meal of her tits.

But my cock threatens to explode in my trousers.

My mouth pulls from her tit with a wet pop.

"On your knees, Red."

Her mouth forms a perfect O.

I smirk and brush my thumb around it, smearing the red lipstick. Soon it will stain my cock.

"Now."

Our gazes remain locked as she lowers to her knees. The erotic sight causes my cock to strain painfully along my thigh. Time for my release.

"Take my dick out."

The red on her cheeks deepens. But she obeys my command. Delicate fingers reach for the placket. They tremble as she opens the closure and lowers the zipper. My trousers drop to the floor, leaving the black boxer briefs. My dick pulses beneath them.

She sucks in a breath.

"Continue."

She nods and slips her fingers in the waistband, then tugs. Slowly, she reveals my v cuts, feathery happy trail, and the tops of my thighs. As the thick base of my cock emerges, she licks her lips.

I groan.

Her eyes flick up to mine. A naughty gleam sparkles in her eyes. The tip of her little pink tongue darts out. She draws it back in extra slow.

I fist her hair and yank.

"Think carefully about teasing me, naughty girl," I chide, then continue. "Take my dick out."

"Yes, Sir."

My heavy balls draw up. I growl.

Quickly, she pulls the boxer briefs down to my ankles. As she lifts her head, I tighten my grip on her hair and fist my cock. She watches as I stroke the girth of my shaft. The bulbous tip an angry red and shiny with pre-cum. I tap it against her lips.

"Open," I growl in a feral voice, more wolf than man.

She mewls as her lips part.

I feed my thick length into her mouth inch by inch until she gags. I push more as I growl for her to relax her throat. Tears trickle down her flushed cheeks. Her fingernails dig into the backs of my thighs. But she obeys. My cock pulses as it stretches her throat. I bite my lower lip on a groan.

"Fuck, Red. You take my dick like a good little girl."

She bobs her head as her eyes shine with pride.

When her nose meets my groin, I hold her still with both hands tangled in her hair. After a few seconds, she pushes against me. I hush her and hold on a bit longer, knowing she can take it.

"Breathe through your nose, like a good little girl."

She swallows.

I groan.

After she relaxes again, I pull out at the same slow pace as I entered. She sputters around my tip as saliva drips from the corners of her mouth.

I praise her some more before I slide back in, faster this time. At the back of her throat, she gags a moment, then remembers to relax. I ease down her throat. This time, I only hold her to me for a moment, then snap my hips back to withdraw. Another snap and I surge forward.

My toes curl as my balls fill with seed while I fuck her face. Her moans vibrate along my shaft, testing my control. But when I see Red reach her fingers between her legs to fuck herself, I lose it. My breath turns ragged. I grow diamond hard in seconds. I take her mouth and throat with pistoning strokes.

Her fingernails form half-moons on my thighs. She gags.

A tremor shoots from the base of my spine to my balls. I throw my head back. My roar reaches the ceiling. The violent climax unleashes thick ropes of my seed into her belly. My fingers dig into her scalp as I try to ground myself. My eyes roll to the back of my head as my knees wobble.

My cock falls from her mouth with a trail of saliva. I drop to the floor and pull her onto my lap. My face buries in her sweat-dampened hair. The scent of cinnamon sugar caramel apples mixes with the pungent aroma of pheromones and musk. I'm in heaven. I breathe her name against the crown of her head.

She wraps her arms around me and burrows closer. Her soft sigh brings a smile to my lips.

The sharp trill of my mobile disturbs our carnal bliss. I groan and dig for it in my trouser pocket. I can't find it. It goes on and on and on…

I wake with a jolt.

Warm, creamy jizz coats my eight-pack abs and pecs.

Glancing around my bedroom, I realize my alarm woke me from a dream. The intense dreams shared by fated mates before they meet or complete their bond. They're like premonitions. Signs you're to meet your fated mate soon. The dreams will only increase in intensity and frequency until the pair fulfills the bond.

Just great.

My inner Dom wants kinks satisfied.

My wolf runs feral.

I'm no closer to a solution.

With a frustrated groan, I roll from the king-size bed and stalk to the en suite bathroom.

How the hell will I get through fifty-nine more days?

CHAPTER 8

ren

"Do. Not. Move."

"If you want this, Red, you better obey."

"On your knees, Red."

"Now."

"Take my dick out."

"Continue."

"Open."

"Breathe through your nose, like a good little girl."

Even though it was only a dream—albeit the most realistic erotic fantasy in history—Mr. Dahl's passionate dominance as he issued filthy commands makes me wet. Again.

He used my mouth without restraint for his carnal pleasure. Ruthless. Unstoppable. Wild.

I loved it.

Every single second of it.

Naked at his feet being used so deliciously, my body thrummed. I was no longer the shy, I'm thankful for what you give me lover. No concern for how my more robust figure appeared. Instead, a part of me I never knew existed rose to the forefront. She relished in his savagery. She sought to please him, to gain his praise—like a good little girl.

Oh, God!

So filthy!

So right.

She wanted more and sought her carnal rhapsody. Her fingers cupped heavy breasts and pinched the nipples, tender from his wickedly skillful mouth. The touches offered a taste of satisfaction but not enough. More!

Fingers trailed down her belly in search of her aching, greedy core. They skimmed over her bare mons and traced her slick seam. A soft cry around his girth resulted in a lusty groan from him. Power raced through her. She controlled this man with her willing mouth. Her confidence soared.

Pleased, she slipped a fingertip between the dripping folds. Still not nearly enough. His fervent thrusts provided a hint to her satisfaction. She mimicked his movements and thrust her fingers deep inside her dripping pussy three times. *Yes! Yes! Yes!* She thought triumphantly. The pads stroked her sensitive G-spot. She shattered in orgasmic bliss.

Her heavy-lidded eyes met his flashing ones. He growled and took her mouth with dominant force. His cum shot straight down her stretched throat to fill her belly like a torrent. No need to swallow.

She watched entranced as a long string of saliva swung between her mouth and his cock when he slipped out. She preened with the knowledge she brought this sexy, dominant man to his knees. Content, she wrapped her arms around him and burrowed against his firm chest with a soft sigh.

Can I be that *good little girl* in real life? For Tag Dahl?

Stop it, Wren Byrd! He is your B-O-S-S. Enough!

Yeah, wistful thinking.

I set my naughty fantasy aside and stare out the window of the Larson Enterprises Mercedes-Benz sedan. Since I left my car in the company's garage yesterday, Beth arranged a second car to bring me to work this morning.

Now, I need to focus on making up for a not-so-great first day. That is, if I can step onto the elevator without fainting.

"Good morning, Beth," I say a bit sheepishly as I approach her desk. My eyes dart past her to the empty office. No sign of Mr. Dahl. I shift my gaze back to her.

She smiles and rises from her leather chair.

"Hi, there, Wren! You look much better. How do you feel today?" She asks as she rounds her desk.

My cheeks heat with embarrassment. I duck my head.

"Aaw, don't let it bother you. Things happen. Now, let's get you settled."

She gestures to the desk opposite hers on the other side of the double doors of Mr. Dahl's office. The desk and chair match the modern decor of his private reception area. The neutral palette of sand, tan, and white appears on the wall and floor treatments and on the furniture. I place my black crocodile handbag on the sand-colored wooden desk while Beth pulls out the matching leather chair.

"Have a seat. I'll help to you log into the network. IT generated your credentials and created your email address," she says as she opens the new laptop. "Remember, the employee handbook states staff cannot use the company's laptop for personal activities. Mr. Dahl is a stickler for protocols. You do not want to get on his bad-bad side, as opposed to his bad side, or the gods forbid his bad-cubed side. You'll learn the scale soon enough."

"Thank you, Beth."

I make a mental note of the stickler part. The beast expects the rules to be followed. Check. I certainly don't want to fall on the worse side of his personality. I prefer him as a teddy bear.

Speaking of which…

"His office is empty. But he told me to be here at nine. Is he in a meeting?"

Beth's fingers hover over the keyboard. She turns her head and eyes me for a moment. Her scrutiny makes me shift in the chair. I lower my gaze to the laptop screen.

"We're all expected to be here at nine. I arrive half an hour earlier just in case Mr. Dahl needs anything unexpectedly. You may want to consider doing the same," she says with an unreadable expression. "As for his where-abouts, he's out of the office at meetings this morning. He'll meet with you at two this afternoon."

It's not so much her words as it is the tone and the subtle implication that make me blush. It's as though she's aware of my against-the-rules attraction to him. Just the thought of his brawny body causes heat to gather in my core. I press my thighs together.

Beth's nose twitches, then her eyes narrow slightly.

The ring of her office phone catches her attention. She hurries to her desk. As she adjusts the headset and talks to the caller, her eyes remain on mine.

I avoid her gaze and busy myself with arranging my desk. From my handbag, I remove the sterling silver frame with a photo of my parents and me on St. Jean Beach in St. Barths. It was one of the happiest times we had before their accident. I want to have the pleasant memory near me as I work to make myself independent of Uncle George.

For a moment, I wonder why I haven't heard from him since I ended the engagement with Jonathan. I'm sure it'll be a big to-do. My spirit sinks at the thought. Then I shake my head. No. I will not allow them to taint my day.

I smile at the photo to dispel the negativity. Warmth envelops me. My heart leaps as I imagine my parents' words of encouragement.

With that positive thought, I reach into my handbag for my writing folder and pen. Others may use iPads or other electronic devices for their planning. But I prefer the old-fashioned pad and pen. I guess it's the artist in me.

I place my handbag on the cabinet behind me. Out of the shopping bag, I lift potted white orchids and set it next to the frame. I take out the other orchids and carry them to Beth's desk. Her eyes widen as I place the flowers on the corner. She's still on the phone, so I smile and return to my desk.

A moment later, she squeals and claps her hands. No longer assessing, her eyes shine as she smiles at me.

"Wren, they're gorgeous. Thank you!"

I smile back and respond, "Orchids are associated with wealth, luxury, and good fortune. They enhance career success. The perfect gift for my new work buddy. At least, I hope we can be friends."

She giggles and walks over with her arms open. I stand for her hug.

"Of course! You know, us girls have to stick together. I love Mr. Dahl to death. But he can be brusque and try me. It'll be good to have someone to share the brunt of his demands and moods. Plus, at lunch, I'll introduce you to Ginny and Dana. They're Mr. Jagger and Mr. Viggo's admins."

She nods toward their office suites.

"But before all of that, let's get you up and running. Then I'll give you a tour of the executive floor. I want you situated before Mr. Dahl arrives. He's not grumpy. We're ecstatic!"

I join in on her giggles.

The morning goes by in a whirl of activity. After the

tour, Beth places a stack of mail in my inbox with a wide grin.

"My gift for you. Or rather, for myself! I won't have to handle Mr. Dahl's social life *and* professional aspects. Those are invitations, letters for donations, so on and so on. He's a popular guy. Everyone wants a piece of him. If you need any help, let me know."

She winks and spins on her high heels. She practically skips to her desk and sits in her chair, crossing her long, toned legs with a flourish. Just as the phone rings. She laughs and mouths, "Busy, busy, busy!"

I giggle and shake my head.

Time to get to work.

So engrossed in organizing the life of an extremely popular billionaire, I startle at the knock on my desk. I glance up to find Beth flanked by two other young women I assume are Ginny and Dana. The trio grins.

"Lunchtime!" They chorus as Beth rolls my chair away from my desk.

I laugh and grab my handbag while she introduces me to the other two. We chat as we head to the elevator. I ignore the twinge in my belly. They glance at me with concern, and I smile. But I wonder how they could tell I was nervous.

The executive elevator opens behind us with a ding.

Mr. Jagger strides out, followed by Mr. Dahl.

My heart flutters as our eyes connect. His emerald greens scan my face before they travel down my body. Section by section, my skin heats beneath his gaze.

"Good afternoon, Mr. Larson, Mr. Dahl."

Beth's greeting draws his eyes from me to her.

I blink and turn to her as she continues.

"You returned earlier than expected. Would you like us to delay our lunch, sir?"

His eyes flick to me briefly.

"No, I have some phone calls to make," he responds, then returns his gaze to me. "Wren, you look better."

"Yes, Mr. Dahl, sir. I feel better, thank you," I all but stutter. To my relief, his face remains stoic.

"Good. Enjoy your lunch. When you return, we will meet to discuss my expectations."

He nods and turns to Mr. Larson, who speaks with Ginny.

I force myself to look away. As a distraction, I pick up the conversation with Dana. Like my namesake bird, I chatter incessantly. Except house wrens usually do so in response to large animals that may be predators. Only humans here, but nervousness causes me to rattle on.

Finally, Ginny rejoins us, and we step onto an arriving elevator. As the doors close, I glance up to find Mr. Dahl watching me. A tug pulls at my heart. I nibble my lower lip.

The doors slide close.

~

*T*AG

. . .

"IF YOU'RE FINISHED OGLING Wren, we can continue our discussion."

I blow a breath and turn away from the elevator. Jagger chuckles.

"You better work on your poker face, bro. Otherwise, the entire office will know you have the hots for your assistant."

He guffaws and slaps me on the shoulder.

If we weren't in the office, I'd wrestle his ass to the ground. Instead, I growl and shake his hand off. My reaction only makes him laugh harder. Damn, the start of day 59 goes from a wet dream to a schoolboy drooling. Jagger is right. I must do better.

We talk as we walk, then part at the entry to my office suite.

"Try not to bang her on the sofa after lunch. You know I like to stretch out on it when I need to think outside of my office suite," he says, chuckling and heads to his offices.

I growl and storm towards the doors to mine. The bouquet of fresh flowers mixes with Wren's scent. It permeates the air and every fiber of my being. My wolf sits on his haunches with a feral grin on his face. I shake my head and step forward.

The glint of silver catches my eye.

I move to her desk and lift the picture frame.

A young Wren—around eight or nine—stands between a man and a woman I assume to be her parents. Their carefree smiles shine brighter than the sun above them. Her facial features resemble a soft, feminine version of her father. She inherited her luxurious mahogany hair and full figure from her mother.

According to her background check, her parents died when she was nine years old. It must have been shortly after they took this photo. They were a lovely family.

My heart clenches as I return the frame to her desk.

It makes me wonder what having a family with Wren would be like. Her belly round with my pups. Going on a beach vacation like her parents. Maybe even a group trip with Jagger, Sage, their twins and Dylan and Sasha with their daughter. Which of us would our pups take after? Would they be able to shift? More importantly, would Wren survive the transition? Hell, would she want it?

My mobile vibrates in my trouser pocket.

I scrub a hand down my face before I answer the call. It's a project manager for a new resort with a major problem. The perfect distraction—work. Finished with the call, I throw myself into the rest of my day's plans with zeal. Anything to not ponder potential impossibilities.

Movement outside my office draws my attention. Wren and Beth stand in the reception area talking to Ginny and Dana. With their backs to me, I soak in Wren.

Her hair piled atop her head shines in the overhead lighting. The exposed column of her neck meets her shoulder. The exact spot for my claiming bite.

My fangs punch through my gums and drip with the serum to bestow the gift. At the thought of making her mine, my cock thickens. As a shower and not a grower, my length remains the same while the girth expands. I have to adjust my cock down my thigh thanks to the instant arousal.

Wren glances over her shoulder, and our eyes meet. I yank my hand from beneath the desk. She blinks and flicks her eyes between my hand and the desk. Again, she bites on that lush lower lip. I growl, wanting to taste the sweet flesh.

Ginny and Dana walk away. Beth heads to her desk, then notices me through the glass wall. She nods and says something to Wren, who also nods. She rushes to her desk. A moment later, the intercom buzzes. I will my fangs to retract then answer with my eyes on her.

"Yes, Wren?"

Her name on my lips makes my cock pulse.

"Uh, Mr. Dahl, sir, it's almost two o'clock. Are we still meeting?"

"Yes, Wren. You may come."

My lips twitch as her cheeks pinken and she stutters an affirmative response. Interesting, she caught the double entendre. I get the sense she's interested in me. But enough to welcome me as her fated mate?

I watch her as she rises from her desk chair and grabs a leather portfolio, pen, her mobile, and a folder. Her grip-worthy hips move with naturally sensuous grace. She's petite, around five feet, four inches. But the fuck-me heels add another four inches to her height. The silk blouse and pencil skirt remind me of the dream.

My cock leaks.

Ordinarily, I would conduct the meeting at the conference table. Given my massive erection, I'll stay put. I gesture to the guest chair opposite my desk.

She perches on the edge and places the portfolio and mobile on the other chair. The folder she balances on her lap as she holds the pen.

To further test my theory, I send a burst of desire through our fledging mate bond. Her pupils dilate as her lips part. The outlines of her plump nipples appear through the silk. She shifts in the chair. The portfolio slips to the floor. She leans over to pick it up. No engagement ring. A fresh development.

I can't resist and leap from the chair. My hand reaches the portfolio at the same time as hers. Our fingers touch. Electricity zaps us. Her hand jerks back. She gasps. I growl. She blinks. Angling my body to avoid poking her in the eye with my stiff cock, I rise and hand the portfolio to her.

Seated behind my desk, I clear my throat. Expectant eyes stare at me. Yeah, Wren Byrd is definitely interested. I smirk.

"Shall we begin?"

CHAPTER 9

 *ren*

"WHAT THE HELL is going on in that little head of yours, Wren?! Or have you lost your mind?! You're just like your father, not wanting to do your part for the family. I arranged this marriage for the betterment of the family. You are the sole heir. After I retire, Byrd Capital cannot cease business because you don't want to marry Jonathan. He's the suitable candidate for the role of CEO. I don't give a damn he was with his neighbor. You will marry Jonathan!"

I bristle at Uncle George's offensive words.

How dare he insult my father and me? It always has to be my uncle's way. Anything else is unacceptable. He's more concerned with a business merger than the bonding of two loves or with Jonathan's infidelity. And if my uncle trained me to run Byrd Capital like I asked so many times, Jonathan wouldn't even be in the picture!

"Wren, I agree with George. Women of our standing do what we must for the family. The idea of princes and glass slippers is unrealistic. You're twenty-five. I was married to George by then, as expected of me. It's time for you to grow up and face your responsibilities."

"Here, Wren, give me your hand."

My head swivels from Wretched Gretchen to Jonathan.

His cold eyes send a chill down my spine. I glance at his raised hand. He holds the engagement ring in his fingers. What the hell?!

"How did you get that? You left it in my condo."

"Don't be daft, Wren. I used my access code. Here. Put it on."

He reaches for my hand.

I jump to my feet and glare at Uncle George.

"No! I will not marry Jonathan! And stop speaking disrespectfully about my parents and me! I've had enough of it!"

I spin on my heels and rush through the living room.

"If you walk out of that door, Wren Byrd, it will remain shut to you forever. You refuse to support this family? This family will no longer support you. You will be on your own. Think very carefully on your next move."

Tears blur my vision now turned red.

Un-fucking-believable!

So be it.

I know my worth, even if they don't.

I straighten my spine and hold my head high then march out of the Fisher Island mansion.

"Wren, Human Resources sent your request for an advance on your salary to me. That's an unusual request. Would you mind explaining the need?"

My face flames red. I wish I could disappear from in front of Mr. Dahl and erase his memory. I had no idea HR would inform him of my appeal.

It's been two weeks since the blowup with George. I refuse to refer to him as an uncle since no blood relative should treat one in the manner he treated me. He made good on his promise to not support me. He closed my bank accounts and my credit cards. I had a few hundred dollars in cash on hand. My condo? Well, I learned Byrd Capital holds the deed. The following morning, I received a forty-eight-hour notice to vacate the premises. Maya came over, and we loaded my necessities into her Mercedes-Benz G-Wagen and my car. Fortunately, the title is in my name. I've been living with her ever since.

Tears fill my eyes. I try to stop them from falling. But it's no use. I bawl. A real ugly cry—sobs, snot, saliva.

Mr. Dahl rushes to my side and hands a handkerchief to

me. He asks questions. But I just shake my head. I'm beyond distraught.

The only saving graces have been my best friend and my job. But I'm no freeloader. I have to contribute for staying with Maya. Even though she tells me no and refuses the money. It's the principle of the matter. But a couple of hundred dollars don't go far, and I've only had one paycheck. I have excellent credit and opened credit cards to help. But I must pay them each month. Not to mention I need a place to live.

The waterworks flow faster.

Suddenly, I'm scooped from the guest chair. My eyes fly open. I'm nose-to-nose with Mr. Dahl. His brows knit together over eyes darkened to jade with worry. Then I hear the rumbling. Its vibrations reverberate through my body. My eyes close on a hiccup. I relax against him as he carries me like I weigh a feather. I open them again when I feel his muscular thighs under my butt. He's sitting on the sofa, and I'm on his lap. Eek!

I squirm to get up. But he growls low in his chest as he tightens his grip. My gaze swings from his face to the glass wall. Thank goodness the privacy shading blocks the office's interior. I'd be mortified if Beth or someone else witnessed me on the boss' lap.

"Do. Not. Move."

I gasp. Those are his exact words and commanding tone from the dream. And I've experienced plenty more erotic fantasies of my boss in the past few weeks.

My head whips towards him.

His eyes flash. An air of dominance emanates from him. I lower my gaze and settle on his lap.

"Now, tell me what happened."

Tag

By the time Wren finishes, my blood boils thick in my veins. My wolf runs, gnashing his teeth and snarling. Who the fuck abandons their own flesh and blood over utter bullshit? It's not as though her uncle couldn't groom her as his successor or hire a trustworthy CEO. Arranged marriages are common, even amongst wolf shifters. But not against the she-wolf's will. Just like Jagger stopped Signy's arrangement.

And to put Wren out on the street with nothing but a few dollars, items, and her car? Thank the gods for her friend Maya. Now, she's someone who's deserving of Wren. Not that fucker Jonathan. The dumbass. He didn't know how to treat Wren. For him and her family to call her names because of her body type? That's nuts! She's perfect. Soft in all the right places. A female who can handle a big male like me.

I shake my head as my cock agrees. No need to give her a reason to jump off my lap. I'd rather she straddles me. Cut it, Dahl!

"I didn't realize HR would inform you of my request.

I'm utterly embarrassed."

Wren hangs her head. A tear drops to her hands folded in her lap.

I capture her chin between my thumb and index finger to turn her head.

"No need for *you* to be embarrassed. It's your uncle who should feel that way. No real man would neglect his family, especially a female. He should cherish and treat you well. Even more so since you lost your parents at such a young age. But don't worry. I'll take care of you."

She blinks in surprise.

I don't. My fated mate needs me. I can't leave her. I won't leave her. She is mine to protect, care for, and to love. Yeah. I'm a goner. Decision made.

She opens her mouth to respond. I put my finger against her lips.

"Go into my private bathroom and wash your face. Then come back here to me."

She nibbles her lower lip.

This time, I lean forward and nip the succulent flesh with my teeth. She gasps. I growl and swat her hip.

"Go."

Her pupils dilate. Her unique scent of cinnamon sugar caramel apples mixes with the musky aroma of her arousal as her desire flares. She jolts when I squeeze her hip. I nod towards the bathroom door. She scrambles from my lap and rushes for the door.

My cock thickens at the sight of her ass jiggling beneath her silk dress.

Mine!

When she disappears behind the door with a furtive glance at me, I smirk and whip out my mobile. Call complete, I rise and put on my suit jacket. My fated mate steps out of the bathroom. Her eyes are red but clear. The color in her cheeks lessened. She smooths her dress and walks over to me.

"Get your bag."

Without hesitation, she scurries for the doors to my office. My inner Dom watches, pleased at her naturally submissive behavior. Oh, the things I will do to her soon. I follow her out and turn to Beth.

"Wren and I have a project. We won't return to the office today. Leave when you're done."

Beth's eyes widen. Then she realizes her faux pas and nods. Surreptitiously, she glances at Wren, who stares at the floor. Crimson colors her cheeks again. The gossip will start for sure now. I no longer give a damn. Wren Byrd is mine.

I place my hand on the small of her back and guide her to the executive elevator. She stops and glances up at me, trepidation in her eyes. Before she can speak, I do.

"Wren, do you trust me?"

Her eyes flick to the elevator and back to me. She nods.

I cock an eyebrow.

"Words, Wren, I will have your words."

A soft breath escapes her parted lips.

"Yes, sir."

My cock pulsates.

"There's My Sweet Girl."

Her mouth-watering tits rise on a deep inhalation. Slowly, the air dispels.

I press the call button. Other than the rumble from my chest, we ride down in silence. I guide her around the corner to the other bank of elevators. The concierge greets us and hands a slip of paper to me. I thank her and head towards the last elevator.

"If you don't mind me asking, where are we going?"

I glance down at my fated mate and smile.

"It's a surprise."

"Okay."

We step onto the elevator reserved for the top levels of The Larson Tower. I press the button for the seventieth floor. A few people join us. I stand behind my fated mate with my hands on her shoulders to ground her. I keep the rumble low so she can feel it, but others can't hear it. She leans against me. I grin like the Cheshire Cat.

We're the last ones off. The doors open to a foyer with two sets of double doors. I gesture for her to step out and guide her to the pair to our left. I glance at the slip of paper and type in the access code. Then step back for her to enter.

"Oh. My. Goodness! This is spectacular!"

She glides over the white marble floors towards the wall of twenty-foot-high windows. The vast Atlantic Ocean serves as the backdrop. She stands in silhouette against its turquoise waters. However, its beauty pales compared to my fated mate. Her eyes glow as she faces me.

"What a surprise! I've never been so high above Biscayne Bay. This view is breathtaking."

She takes my breath away. I put my hands in my trouser pockets to prevent them from pulling her into my arms. Instead, I turn and nod at the rest of the space.

"The view is only part of the surprise. This, My Sweet Girl, is your new residence."

Her mouth falls open. She spins from the windows. Her eyes dart around the oversized living room, entry, towards the stairs, and back to me.

"No way."

"Yes way. Come, I'll give you a tour."

I extend my elbow to her. She stares at it then up at me. I wait. She has to make the move of acceptance. She takes a deep breath and loops her arm through mine. My grin widens.

Hers grows as she takes in the three bedroom suites, four bathrooms, chef's eat-in kitchen, dining room, media room, and office. We return to the living room and sit on a leather sofa, facing the panoramic view.

My fated mate sits too far away from me. I slide over to her side. She watches me but doesn't move. Good girl.

"Thank you for thinking about me, Mr. Dahl. I truly appreciate it. But I cannot afford this condo. Not even with an advance on my salary."

She laughs softly.

"And speaking of salary, I need to return to work. Earn my keep and all," she adds as she rises.

My hand shoots out and clasps her wrist. She startles.

"Wren, I don't expect you to pay for it. This is one of Larson Enterprises' corporate condos. They're used by visitors. So, there's no fee. You can stay here for as long as you like. Give you time to get acclimated to supporting yourself. And you'll save on gas."

The corners of her mouth quirk up at my lame joke. However, she shakes her head.

"I can't possibly accept your gracious offer, Mr. Dahl. I left one situation dependent on someone. It's not possible for me to put myself in the same situation again. But I thank you."

I growl in frustration. Why can't I get her to see it's for the best without freaking her out about being my fated mate? I can close multibillion-dollar deals. But words escape me with Wren. Think quick, Dahl!

"Sit a moment."

She pauses, then lowers herself to the sofa. Our knees brush. That zing of electricity sparks between us. She gasps. It's my opening.

I take her hands in mine. Go for it, Dahl.

"Wren, I'm going to be honest with you," I start and wait for her eyes to meet mine. "I know you are my social assistant and company policy forbids a personal relationship between a manager and a subordinate. But I can't help my attraction to you. It's natural. Something I can't stop. Something I don't want to stop."

I pause to gauge her reaction. She remains still.

"You feel it too. Don't you?"

She hesitates, then nods. I cock an eyebrow.

"Yes, Mr. Dahl, sir."

I shake my head.

"Tag, Wren, call me Tag."

"Yes, Tag."

"I propose you end your employment contract with Larson—"

She sucks in a breath and frees her hands from mine. Shaking my head, I grab them back before she stands.

"Let me finish," I say, and she stills. "I propose you end your employment contract with Larson Enterprises *and* sign an independent contractor agreement with me. The only changes would be the elimination of the non-fraternization and sixty-day trial clauses and an increase in your pay to allow for health insurance coverage. The agreement would include the condo too."

My fated mate purses her lips.

"That office you gushed about would be *your* office. And when I need to entertain guests for dinners and such as you think makes sense for my social endeavors, you can host the events here. Until you find a place you prefer, you live here too. It's a win-win situation. You maintain your independence with a generous package and a place to live and I keep my social assistant with no barriers to us exploring our mutual attraction."

I squeeze her hands.

"What do you think?"

My fated mate studies my face. I keep an open expression, so she won't find any deceit. She nods, then her eyes rove around the living room.

My wolf senses pick up her increased heart rate and her excitement. I wait patiently, knowing she'll accept my offer.

She purrs.

"Shall we begin?"

CHAPTER 10

 *ren*

I FALL into the dark green depths of Tag's eyes as he stares at me with unabashed, blatant hunger. What a moment ago was a soothing rumble morphs into a carnal growl. Erotic energy swirls around us, replacing the zaps of electricity at our innocent touches. My heart races as he holds me in a sexual thrall.

"Think carefully about teasing me, naughty girl."

"I wouldn't dream of it, Sir."

Tag jumps from the sofa with an animalistic grace. His feral eyes focus on me. Seconds later, I hang upside-down over his shoulder. I squeal and wiggle to get free of his hold. A spank to my ass stills me.

"Behave. Naughty. Girl," he says punctuating each word with a spank.

My pussy clenches. I moan wantonly.

"Where are you taking me?" I pant.

He jogs up the stairs two at a time. I bounce and grab his waist. His grip under my butt tightens.

"To spread you out on the bed and feast on you for hours. If you're a good little girl."

My pussy gushes. A long, low moan slips from my mouth.

Oh, God!

So filthy!

So right.

Perhaps I can be that *good little girl* in real life for Tag Dahl, after all. But will he accept my extra-curvy figure naked, like in my fantasies? My heart lurches at the thought he'll wrinkle his nose in disgust like Jonathan's neighbor or call me names like he did. I hope—

"OWEE!! Wh—What was that for?"

Tag's palm rests on my stinging butt cheek. The heat from the spank radiates from the spot. The sting follows.

"Stop thinking so hard, naughty girl."

I fly through the air. Arms and legs flail. With an oomph, I land amongst fluffy pillows on the king-size bed. I rise on my elbows and toss my hair out of my face. My eyes narrow on Tag, then half-mast at the sight of him stripping.

He doesn't say a word, just keeps his eyes locked on mine. The suit jacket drops from his broad shoulders. He tosses it to the sofa. Maintaining eye contact, he crouches and unties his shoes. He stands and toes them off. One knee after the other bends to remove the socks. He places gold cufflinks on the table and pulls the dress shirt from his trousers.

I sit up, not wanting to miss the reveal of his chest. My teeth draw my lower lip into my mouth.

He shakes his head and stalks towards me. He crawls from the foot of the bed up my body. I hold my breath. His thumb rests on my lower lip, then pulls it from between my teeth. He leans over and licks the plump flesh. I mewl.

Eyes still on mine, he reverses his crawl and stands. His fingers loosen the silk tie. He tosses it over his shoulder towards the sofa. Neither of us bother to check where it landed. Slowly, methodically, he unbuttons his shirt. The sides flap open. I growl in disappointment at the white undershirt blocking my view. He chuckles wickedly.

He grips it behind his neck and yanks the offensive garment over his head. The undershirt drifts to the floor. I'd say good riddance. But the air whooshes from my lungs, leaving me breathless.

What I imagined being a muscular chest proves I'm not so creative. He's magnificent. Carved like Adonis with his v cuts, eight-pack abs furrowed to perfection, and his chiseled pecs with paw-print tattoos on each one. Who would expect this serious man to have not one but two tattoos? A bad boy in disguise? I'll take him. Thank you!

Bulging biceps flex as he reaches for the leather belt at his narrow waist. I lean forward with my tongue hanging out in anticipation of his next reveal. Judging by the thick length along his thigh, he won't disappoint.

Again, he chuckles. The smirk on his face is well deserved. The pants drop to the floor. Outlined beneath black boxer briefs is a log. It twitches, and I jump. Fingers trace the length and circle the head. I blink to be sure I didn't imagine the moisture on the boxer briefs near the tip of his cock. No, it's there.

Oh, God!

My thighs press together as my core aches to be filled to the max by him.

He tilts his head back with nostrils flared. His abs tighten as he inhales deeply. A growl slips from his mouth on the exhalation. Intense eyes flash.

My fingers bunch the duvet, and my toes point when he strips the last article of clothing from his body. His ginormous cock springs free. It points directly at me. The tip glistens. My tongue darts out to lick my lips.

I groan deep in my throat as he fists the base of his dick, strokes up, then tugs the plum-shaped head. More cream leaks from the slit. His sac swings like a pendulum.

My eyes sweep across the muscular planes of this real-life Adonis. I hum my appreciation.

"You like my body?"

I nod vigorously, then add a few verbal yes, Sirs.

"I like yours. Now, show me."

My jaw drops, flabbergasted.

No. No. No. Me? Stand and strip for him? Ah, no.

I switch my gaze to the floor-to-ceiling windows.

Sunlight streams inside, bathing the room in brightness. Not even a shadow to hide my flaws. Never have Jonathan and I had sex in a room so lit up. It was at night with the blackout shades drawn and maybe a couple of flickering candles in the corner. This? No.

So caught up in sheer panic, I don't notice the bed shift as Tag sits beside me. I squeak when he cups my face and turns it towards him.

"Wren, you are a beautiful female with a sinful body a man like me worships from your head to your toes. You're my own lush playground. I want to lose myself in you. Bring you pleasures you never knew existed. Make you cum on my tongue, on my fingers, on my cock. Mark you in every way as mine. Do you understand?"

Now, my jaw drops for another reason. To hear a man say such beautiful things amazes me. A man like Tag Dahl? Floors me.

I study his face for any artifice. Only eyes full of honesty stare back at me. Even my heart warms as though he touched deep within me. Relief floods my overwrought system.

On a sigh, I nod.

He raises an eyebrow.

The corners of my mouth lift as I respond verbally.

"There's My Sweet Girl. Now, strip so I can feast."

I scamper off the bed. Then yelp when he spanks my butt. I rub the spot as I glance over my shoulder. He winks and stretches out on the bed with his cock tall like a flagpole. My mouth waters. I forget my body issues and the sting.

With a deep breath, I draw on my inner vixen and put on what I hope is a sexy striptease. My prayers are answered. When my black silk thong lands atop the matching bra and my dress, Tag throws his head back and howls. His eyes land on me full of savage hunger.

Once again, he sounds more wild animal than a man.

I shiver. Goosebumps spread over my exposed skin. At the same time, red-hot sparks skitter across my body, igniting white-hot passion. Nipples pucker and core clenches. Slick coats my inner thighs. My arousal wafts to my nose. The musky scent makes me wetter. Needier. A whine rises in the back of my throat.

"Come to me, mate."

My knees turn to jelly at Tag's guttural command. Quick as lightning, he leaps from the bed and catches me. Powerful arms carry me to the bed. He uses his knees to reach the center and lays me down. He stares at me with a sensual, possessive, fierce expression. An internal furnace heats me up.

I cup his stubbled cheek. My thumb brushes across his full lips. He sucks it into his mouth and nips the tip. I gasp as erotic tingles shoot up my arm. Then moan as he trails open-mouthed kisses in their wake. My eyes flutter close.

A shudder rolls over me when he reaches the sensitive juncture of my shoulder and neck. He pauses and licks the spot. I angle my head to give him better access. He growls his approval. Warm moisture trickles down my back. He jerks his head away and sits up. My eyes snap open.

"Tag? Are you all right?"

With his face averted, he answers a gruff yes.

I ache to see him and take his face between both hands. He lets me turn his head. I sit up and kiss the closed eyelids. His ragged breath tickles my neck. I kiss every inch of his handsome face. But he remains rigid. My hands glide to his tense shoulders and knead them as I brush my lips over his closed mouth.

"Fuck, Wren."

He bands his arms around me and rolls me beneath him. His enormous body covers me. It blankets me in his heat. His mouth devours mine. He swallows my moans while groans of his own fill my ears. He kisses me breathless, then presses his forehead to mine.

"Tell me yes, Wren. Just say yes, baby. Please."

His eyes filled with anguish and yearning plead with me.

I don't know what he wants me to say yes to. But at this point, I'll give this man whatever he wants. He's treated me better than anyone since my parents. No judgement. No disappointment. No disgust. Instead, he's cared for me, considered my needs, and provided solutions. And the attraction? I feel it as intensely as he does. I yearn for him too.

"Yes, Tag, yes, yes, yes."

"Oh, gods," he groans as his eyes squeeze shut.

I press kisses to his face and murmur soothing words as I caress his back.

His eyes open. A wild glow rises from their dark green depths.

"I really need you, baby. Bare, with nothing between us. I need to take you rough now. After, I'll be gentle. I promise. Okay?"

"Yes."

He growls.

His knee wedges between my legs. Eagerly, I spread them. A finger strokes my soaked seam. He growls and fists his cock. The head slips along my lower lips, collecting the juices. His hips snap back and surge forward. His tremendous girth breaches my folds. I keen from the thick invasion. His tip hits my cervix. I buck.

"Hold on to me, baby."

I wrap around him like a monkey, all arms and legs.

He planks above me on his toes with one hand around my waist and the other gripping the headboard. I don't know what to make of the position until he starts to move. And by God does he.

Thrusts like a speeding locomotive pound me into the mattress. He withdraws to his tip and slams back in. Our groins crash. Skin slaps against skin. His sac smacks the underside of my butt cheeks. He's raw and single-minded.

I love it!

I scream his name as a toe-curling orgasm takes me by surprise. The first I ever had with penetration. Already Tag gives me pleasure I never knew existed. Another one rolls on its heels. Turning the aftershocks into never-ending electrical currents. I cry out, thrashing my head from side to side. My inner walls clamp on his magical cock, greedily wanting more.

He bellows. His grueling pace increases. The headboard slams against the wall. Our bodies—slick with sweat—slip and slide with his forceful thrusts. His grunts and growls fill the room. The scent of primal sex surrounds us. It's animalistic fucking.

I hiss from the stretch and burn of his ginormous cock in my tight pussy. It hurts oh so good. Then his cock swells. It grows impossibly larger. I moan as it drives deeper into my ravaged core.

Without stopping, he takes my hands and raises them above my head. Palms press to the headboard. He twines our fingers and buries his face in my neck. Sharp teeth graze my throat. My back bows from the bed. Every cell in my body explodes from carnal desire. I want this man to possess me.

"YES!!!"

I scream without being asked a question. My body knows an answer is due.

Tag roars.

His mouth leaves my neck. He rears back on his haunches, yanking me with him. I straddle his muscular thighs. He grips the back of my neck with one hand and wraps the other arm around my waist. Securing me to his body. He pumps up into me once, twice, then slams me down. He grinds against me, burrowing his dick to the root. Like a geyser, his cock spurts his release in a series of scorching spasms.

Another orgasm blows my mind. I throw my head back and cry out in wild abandon.

~

*T*AG

F*UCK*. Me.

First, I call her mate.

Then, I almost issue the claiming bite. Not once. But twice in only round one of making love.

Wren drives me to lose all control.

My wolf roared in frustration when I held back. Hell, I roared along with him. The urge so strong to make her mine nearly undid me.

But I need her permission. And she needs to understand what it all means, including the risks. Not to mention Jagger will lose his shit if I claim Wren unbeknownst to her.

I scrub a hand down my face and peer at her between the fingers.

She lies sated, blissfully unaware of my inner turmoil. Her cheeks flushed and lips kiss swollen. Her tousled hair spreads out on the pillow. I have the most gorgeous fated mate. And she doubts her beauty. That dumb fuck

Jonathan. But if he hadn't been a moron, I may never have met my fated mate.

She's agreed to my proposal, told me yes without knowing what I wanted, and most of all, she trusts me.

I will not allow a lack of self-control to ruin us before we even get started. I have time. No. We have time. And I won't muck it up.

"THAT'LL DO IT. You're officially an independent contractor specializing in social engagements and event planning with me as your first client. Congratulations, Wren!"

Tag grins and hands me the countersigned agreement and my corporation documents.

In less than twenty-four hours, he arranged for Larson Enterprises' legal department to write up and to file the necessary paperwork. He's determined to get me situated quickly.

Which is why we're in his office with the head of the department on a Saturday afternoon. I'm sure she'd rather spend her weekend doing something more fun than explaining legalese to me.

I smile at her gratefully, then turn my gaze to Tag.

"Thank you. Thank you both so much. This is beyond exciting!"

"You're welcome and good luck to you, Wren," she says and turns to Tag. "If you don't require any further assistance, I'll take my leave."

"No. Thank you."

She smiles and leaves.

As I watch, the glass wall darkens. I turn to Tag.

He's staring at me with hooded eyes filled with carnal desire. I shiver as he rises and takes my hand.

Wordlessly, he leads me to the conference table, places my palms on its surface, pulls my hips back to lengthen my torso over the table, and flips my dress up. He kicks my legs to spread them. I oblige and widen my stance. His hands caress my butt cheeks bare since I don't have any panties on.

Automatically, my back arches and lifts my butt higher into his hands.

He growls in appreciation, then squeezes each mound and pulls them apart. His growl deepens as he stares at my exposed rear.

My head jerks around.

His flashing eyes lift to mine.

"I will claim each of your holes, including your ass. But not today. You must build up the ability to accommodate my size like a good little girl."

My forehead drops to the table with a thud as I moan.

He chuckles wickedly as my juices trickle to the floor.

Then his mouth is on me. I buck against him. With a chastising growl, he grips my undulating hips to still them. He devours my pussy like a ravenous man, grunting and groaning with carnal satisfaction.

I lose count of the orgasms. One follows the other for endless pleasure. My entire body shakes. Incoherent cries of passion pour from my mouth in pants. Just as my juices gush down Tag's throat.

He rises, smacks each butt cheek, and thrusts his massive cock inside of my quivering core. It contracts around him, squeezing like a vise. He growls barbarically.

"You like how my big cock claims every inch of your little pussy?" His voice thrums in my ear.

My palms slap the table as I respond with a garbled cry.

"I'll take that as a yes. So, I'll give you more."

He withdraws slowly. I feel every ridge, every vein, and every inch of his dick. I mewl, then scream when he slams back in with one brutal thrust. It lifts me to the tips of my toes and pushes the edge of the table into my pelvis. Another long, slow stroke followed by another slam, again and again until I'm a spluttering, wet mess.

"Cum for me once more, like a good little girl."

I shake my head, too sensitive for more.

He licks the side of my sweaty neck.

"Yes. You. Will."

The last stroke sends me over the edge. I cum screaming like a banshee, shaking violently beneath him.

He roars and fills my core to overflowing with his hot, creamy seed. His thrusts slow down to a lazy place, gently slapping his groin against my ass. He lowers his torso to my back. I moan softly as he trails kisses along my neck.

"I've had the fantasy of fucking you on this table for the longest time."

Oh, God!

*T*AG

"I'M glad I could get my things from the office and leave a note for Beth. I didn't want to disappear without letting her know what happened. It's so sweet you'll keep my orchid on your coffee table."

"It will remind me of you while I'm in my office all alone, without my hot assistant to make the day more enjoyable."

My fated mate giggles and shakes her head.

"I can't wait for you to meet Maya. She's not just my personal trainer, but my best friend. It's thanks to her I embrace my body—"

"*I* want to embrace your body."

She nudges my shoulder and rolls her eyes.

After a quick shower in my private bathroom and I changed out of my suit, we head to Maya's condo to get Wren's things. I'm looking forward to meeting her best friend. Wren speaks so highly of her, and she stood by my fated mate when others abandoned her. I owe Maya my allegiance.

We leave Downtown Miami Bayfront and head to South Beach. As we cross MacArthur Causeway, we pass Moon Island—the Miami Wolves Pack's private island in Biscayne Bay, across from South Beach.

I long to move my fated mate into my bayfront mansion. But we don't allow humans on the island. It's our enclave where we can live in our wolf forms unencumbered. The natural landscape of Moon Island provides protection from unwanted eyes. Then Sage—our Luna and Jagger's fated mate—cast a spell to obscure the island even more. She's the High Witch and Coven of the South leader with remarkable magick, even more so since her mating with Jagger.

For the time being, I'll have to be satisfied with my fated mate living above my office suite in the residential portion of The Larson Tower. Soon, she'll be with me in our home. If she accepts me as a wolf shifter, that is. Not wanting to dwell on it, I tune back in to her ramblings.

I steer my Rolls-Royce Black Badge Wraith onto Ocean Drive. Maya's condo isn't far from the beachfront building where the pack bachelors live. I'm glad I don't see any of them out and about, especially Viggo. He'll enjoy teasing me nonstop. Once things settle with Wren, I'll introduce her to the pack. Not before.

"There. That's Maya's building."

I park and help my fated mate from the coupe. She giggles when I lift her from the seat and plant a kiss on her lips. I stand her up and close the door, then take her hand. She directs me to the private elevator. On the ride up, she smiles at me and squeezes my hand. Her eyes sparkle. I grin. My wolf struts.

The elevator doors open directly into the condo. A stunning human female squeals and rushes towards us. Her jet black hair flows behind her. She throws her arms around my fated mate. They giggle and dance around.

I slip my hands in the pockets of my low-slung joggers and watch their exuberant greeting. But Maya doesn't forget I'm there. She loops her arm through Wren's and faces me. Topaz eyes pin me with a no-nonsense stare. She extends her hand.

"I'm Maya Alejandra Perez Garcia and Wren's best friend," she says as I shake her hand. "She tells me you treat her well. Good. However, should you fuck with my best friend, I will have your balls, Tag Dahl. Got it?"

"Yes, ma'am," I respond, biting back a chuckle, then I turn serious. "I thank you for being a best friend to Wren. Her family did her wrong. But you stood by her. Wren is extremely important to me. I owe you my allegiance."

Maya assesses me for a moment. She nods.

"Excellent. Welcome to my home, Tag," she says with a smile.

"Thank you," I respond, grinning.

I follow the girls through the palatial duplex penthouse. Wren tells me she and Maya will gather her things so I can wait in the living room. Maya offers me something to drink and gestures towards the wraparound terrace. I decline a beverage and head outside. I call the movers and answer work emails while I wait.

After a while, Wren pokes her head out the door and tells me they're ready. I kiss the crown of her head and wrap my arm around her shoulders. They piled boxes in front of the service elevator. I send a text message to the movers. They come upstairs. In no time, they have the boxes loaded on their van. I send a text message to the concierge to tell him to allow the movers access to Wren's duplex.

She rides with Maya back to The Larson Tower. I follow.

I call Jagger and tell him about the latest developments. He's fine with them and agrees it's a good idea to separate Wren from the company because of the non-fraternization policy. We end the call as I pull into the garage.

It's amazing the girls still chatter on. I shake my head and follow them to the elevator. Once again, I'm told they'll take care of everything. I don't mind. At. All.

The concierge stocked the kitchen with Wren's favorite foods and the wet bar with my preferred liquors. I pour two fingers of Macallan Scotch into a Baccarat tumbler and head to the media room to watch basketball.

"There you are! I thought you left."

My fated mate appears in the doorway. Maya peers over her shoulder.

"You won't get rid of me that easily, babe," I say as I stand and stride towards them. "Did you finish everything?"

Her cheeks pinken. Maya giggles.

"Oh, you're good, Tag!" She says.

I bow, sweeping my arms wide.

They burst into giggles.

"Well, if you're done, how about we order some dinner? Binge on Netflix. You know, whatever you two do on a night in."

They glance at each other and double over laughing. They laugh so hard tears slip down their cheeks and snorts mix with their giggles. I can't help but join in.

"Not just good. But *really* good!" Maya chokes out, dabbing her glittering eyes.

"Told ya!" My fated mate says and turns to grin at me.

My heart soars. Then doubt emerges.

Gods, let her accept me and be mine forever.

I snap out of it when she wraps her arms around my neck—standing on tiptoe—and presses her lips to mine. I envelop her in an embrace. Lifting her from the floor, I swing her around.

"You better believe it, Wren Byrd! And never forget it!"

Maya claps.

I put my fated mate down and drape my arm over her shoulders.

"So, what'll it be? Whatever's your favorite spot, I'll get them to deliver."

They start rattling off different restaurants, narrowing down to two. Then turn to me for my preference. Of course, I go along with my fated mate. Maya throws her hands up.

"Now, you're not so good, Tag!" She huffs as her arms fold across her chest.

I grin, and respond, "How about we order from both places? I don't believe in limits."

My eyes drift to Wren. Hopefully, she'll have an open mind when it comes to me being a wolf shifter and her being my fated mate. Not to mention her transition.

"Great idea! Lucky for you, you bounced back to my good side."

I chuckle and whip out my mobile to place our orders. The girls settle on the sofa and switch from my basketball game to Netflix. I don't mind. I sit next to Wren with a grin on my face. It even stays in place as they start some historical romance series called *Bridgerton*.

Viggo would have a field day.

But it's okay. I'll rack up points wherever I can get them. I add her best friend approves of me to the list. When the time is right, I'll have the conversation with my fated mate. For now, I'll make her fall in love with me.

CHAPTER 12

ren

"By the gods, I'm the luckiest male in the world."

I glance over my shoulder to find Tag leaning against the doorframe of the bedroom suite I converted into a dressing room.

He included a stipend for clothing and accessories in our agreement when I told him I wasn't able to bring my gowns and such from the Brickell condo. And I'm glad he did since tonight we attend the most important gala on the Miami social calendar. Plus, it's our first engagement as a couple and I'll meet Jagger and Sage as Tag's girlfriend. With Byrd Capital as a sponsor, George and Gretchen will be in attendance. Jonathan will probably show up, not wanting to miss an opportunity for networking.

Butterflies flutter in my belly.

I place a palm on it atop the silver sequined stretch-tulle gown. I'm glad Tag likes it. It makes me feel sexy. Although strapless, boning in the fitted bodice offers support for my ample bosom. From the fitted and draped waist, the gown falls loosely at the hip to pool on the floor. My leg plays peekaboo through the thigh-high slit. Strappy stilettos lengthen my leg and add height to my petite frame.

"Don't be nervous. You look gorgeous."

Silent like a predator, Tag slipped behind me. His arms encircle my waist, placing his hands over mine. He stares at me through the reflection in the full-length mirror.

I lean into his body, drawing from his strength.

"Thank you. I must say, you wear a mean tux, Mr. Dahl. So debonair!"

He smirks.

"Thank you, Ms. Byrd," he responds, then kisses the crown of my head and steps back. "However, you're missing something."

My eyebrows knit together as I face him.

His eyes sparkle like the jewel they resemble as he bites his lush lower lip. He reaches for a shopping bag next to his black patent leather dress shoe.

I recognize the gold logo for an Italian jewelry atelier.

He withdraws a large flat box and holds it out to me. I glance up at him. He cocks an eyebrow. My fingertip presses the gold closure. The lid lifts to reveal a ruby and diamond suite. I gasp at the magnificent matching brooch, earrings, necklace, and bracelet. The flawless gemstones sparkle like fire and ice.

"Rubies signify love, commitment, passion, protection, and wealth. All that I offer you along with my heart forever, My Sweet Girl."

Tears blur my vision.

Tag sets the box on the center island and sweeps me into his arms. He buries his face in my hair and inhales deeply, then murmurs words of love. I clutch him tightly. He holds me until I calm.

"Come, let's rinse your face."

I nod and let him lead me to the en suite bathroom. He puts a towel over my gown and moistens a washcloth with cool water. Carefully, he dabs my face. Fortunately, I always wear waterproof mascara. The rest of my makeup I fix quickly. He stands by and smiles encouragingly.

When I'm done, he takes my hand again. He puts the necklace on me while I slip the earrings and bracelet on. I turn to the oval mirror and clip the brooch to my hair, swept up at the back of my head. The piece is perfect for an exit statement. I face Tag.

"*Bellissima!*"

"*Grazie, amore mio.*"

He grins and drapes the gown's matching cape over my shoulders. I loop my arm through his, and we leave the duplex.

Jagger and Sage's limousine pulls up just as Tag and I

exit The Larson Tower. A second SUV stops behind it. I glance at Tag questioningly, and he tells me it's security. I nod in understanding. Two multibillionaires and me dripping in millions of dollars' worth of jewels need a troop!

A security team member steps from the passenger's side of the limo and opens the door with a nod. Tag nods back. Jagger calls for Tag to get in first, so I don't mess up my gown. The guard helps me inside. I smile at a beautiful woman a few years older than me who must be Sage as I sit beside her. Jagger and Tag sit opposite us.

"Sage Larson Waters, I'd like to introduce you to Wren Byrd, my girlfriend. Wren, this is Sage, Jagger's wife."

I smile and extend my hand to her.

"It's a pleasure to meet you, Mrs.—"

"Oh Wren, no need to be formal. Call us Jagger and Sage," she says with a warm smile. Her emerald green eyes glow against her toffee complexion. "You're radiant. I love your gown and jewels!"

I stare at the robin's egg size diamond pendant dangling from a diamond necklace she wears with other pieces and smile.

"And I love yours too!"

She giggles as her gaze flicks to her husband. He smiles at her lovingly. She faces me.

"Jagger just gifted them to me tonight," she says, as a blush rises on her cheeks. He chuckles, and her cheeks redden further.

As I glance at the smirk on Jagger's handsome face, I get

the sense she thanked him very well. My gaze shifts to Tag. He winks at me. Yeah, I'll thank him equally well later.

"Tell me about your new business, Wren. I could use your help for events I have coming up for my luxury custom-made jewelry company, Sage's Gems & Jewels."

I snap my fingers.

"Now, I know why you look familiar! I read about you in the latest issue of *Ocean Drive Magazine*. I'd love to work with you!"

We chat about her upcoming collection and the events until the limo stops at the gala's venue. We step out from both doors. The guys follow us. Tag holds out his arm, and I slip my hand around it. We follow Sage and Jagger up the red carpet.

Cameras flash and the paparazzi call our names. I fall into my socialite persona—slight smile, perfect posture, measured steps. We pose in front of the step and repeat banner where the Larson Enterprises, Inc. logo appears beside Byrd Capital.

As I smile for the cameras, my gaze flicks around the sea of people. I don't spot George or Gretchen. They must be inside.

Tag leans over and murmurs in my ear, "Don't worry about your uncle and aunt. I won't let them upset you."

I squeeze his arm and whisper my thanks. He beams at me.

We move inside, where we greet people we know. Tag introduces me as his girlfriend to anyone I'm unfamiliar with. Some women respond cordially while others appraise me. Whenever I feel uncomfortable, Tag guides us away and tells me how beautiful I am.

He makes me feel adored. How I love this man. And it is love. My heart warms. When we return to the duplex, I'll tell him just how I feel.

Before the cocktail hour ends, Sage and Jagger approach us. They make a striking couple with their opposite appearances. Her long ebony hair to his short white blond cut. Warm emerald green eyes to chilly ice blue. Petite and curvy to imposing and muscular. As they pass, people watch in admiration.

"Wren, I'm going to the powder room. Would you care to join me?"

Jagger shakes his head.

"One day, you'll explain to me why females go to the bathroom in pairs."

"When you find out, tell me, bro!"

Sage and I ignore their chuckles and head to the powder room to freshen up. We enter the anteroom and check our reflections in the mirrors above the vanities. Voices from the interior reach us.

"And to think he's with her. Again."

"Of all the fabulous women in Miami, he has *her* on his arm?"

"Oh, please! There must be a reason."

They giggle.

The hairs on the back of my neck rise. Instinct tells me

the women refer to Tag and me. I know I've gotten looks at other events we've attended. But we weren't arm-in-arm like we are tonight. Now, they bare their vicious claws.

I turn to leave. But Sage catches my arm.

Her narrowed eyes blaze. She shakes her head.

"Do not allow them to run you off, Wren. Nothing they say is true. They're spiteful and jealous. Come on."

She hooks arms with me and marches to the main part of the powder room. The three women notice us. Malice covers their faces.

"Wren, look who we have here. Moe, Larry, and Curly. The three stooges dressed in last season's collections from the dustbin. How sad they don't have your beauty and grace. Pity. Perhaps then they could've snagged Tag. Ah, well, too late. Let's return to our devoted and loving men, shall we?"

We spin on our heels, leaving the three stooges with their mouths hanging to the floor.

In the hallway, we bust out laughing.

"Did you see their faces?"

"Cracked and on the ground!"

We continue laughing as we approach the ballroom. Then the smile falls from my face.

Tag

. . .

"You know now is a great time for a resort in—"

My chest tightens. Something is wrong. Anxiously, I glance around for my fated mate. I spot her with Sage. Okay. But on closer inspection, I see her uncle and aunt and a guy in front of them. Fuck no!

I charge through the crowd, ignoring Jagger's call. I sense him following me. Then his curse as he sees the direction I'm heading.

My enhanced hearing picks up my fated mate's cry when that fucker yanks her arm. Oh, hell no! Rage like I've never experienced courses through every cell of my being. Adrenaline pumps through me. My wolf snarls and claws beneath my skin. Enraged, my red vision tunnels on the guy.

"Get your fucking hand off her!"

My bellow causes heads to turn. I ignore them and launch myself at him. We crash to the floor. My fists pummel his face. Snarls rip from my throat. His blood flies with each punch landed. The sickening crunch of bone doesn't satisfy me. My wolf wants to tear his throat out. As do I.

Multiple arms grab me from behind and hoist me up. I fight with all my strength to break free. My tunnel vision still focuses on the fucker. He lies on the floor unmoving. But it's not enough. He. Touched. My. Fated. Mate. MINE!

My wolf breaks the surface.

Then I black out.

~

WREN

"WHAT DO you think you're doing, Wren?! You keep showing up at events with Tag Dahl. What does a man like him want with you? You better not smear the Byrd name with your shenanigans!"

George's angry tirade on the heels of those nasty women's comments makes my moment of happiness plummet. And to castigate me in front of Sage makes it worse. I'm so embarrassed I could fall through the floor. And then the door to the powder room closes behind me. Snickers let me know the women heard what he said.

I freeze as flashbacks of George and Gretchen berating me hit me over and over.

Sage says something. But I don't hear her.

A tug on my arm snaps me out of the fog.

Jonathan's angry face is inches from mine. His fingers dig into the tender flesh of my inner arm. He yanks me, and I stumble with a cry.

"Hey! Stop it!" Sage exclaims.

"Get your fucking hands off her!"

Tag runs over with an expression of pure rage. He collides with Jonathan and knocks him to the ground. Straddling him, Tag punches his face repeatedly.

Gretchen screams. George pulls her away and watches from a distance. His cold eyes glare at me as though it's my fault.

I shake my head and turn back to Tag. He continues to beat an unconscious Jonathan until the security team member and others pull Tag off him. Tag tries to fight free. But they hold him firm. Then his features shift. I frown, confused. He looks like—

"Wren, come with me."

A mountain of a man blocks my view. I try to get around him, needing to see what happened to Tag's face. But the man moves with me, then turns me around. I hit his chest with my clutch.

"Get off me! Let me get to Tag!"

Jagger appears.

"Wren, this is Blake. He will take you home. Go. Now."

For some reason, I'm compelled to obey Jagger's command. I nod and let Blake guide me down the hallway, away from Tag and the commotion. When I glance over my shoulder, Blake blocks my view again. He increases his pace to where I have to jog beside him. He keeps a firm hold of my arm and waist to prevent me from falling.

We hurry through the lobby and out the revolving doors. He puts me in the back of the SUV and jumps into the driver's seat. As we pull away from the curb, I shift in my seat to glimpse any sign of Tag. Nothing appears out of the ordinary, nor do I hear police sirens. I watch until the SUV turns a corner, and the venue disappears from view.

As I straighten in the seat, tears fall. I can't make any sense of what I saw happen to Tag's face. It appeared his bones were realigning. His eyes changed to that deeper shade of jade. But somehow appeared animalistic. Almost unrecognizable.

And the strength he possessed and the ferocity. He was unhinged!

My God, have I fallen in love with a madman?

CHAPTER 13

ag

"WHAT THE FUCK, Tag?! You almost shifted in front of humans! I get you were upset about Wren. But to lose *all* control?! You beat that guy unconscious and shifted. Thank the gods Sage was there. Or we'd all be screwed. Total chaos."

Jagger has every right to be pissed.

I screwed up big time.

Never ever in my entire life has rage consumed me. It blinded me to all except that fucker with his hands on Wren. My. Fated. Mate. My female touched by another male and in a rough manner? Hell no!

I don't regret breaking his face one bit. He deserved it. To mistreat Wren verbally and mentally was bad enough.

She left him, and she's now with me. But he touched her. Physically yanked her arm hard enough to make her cry out. Unacceptable. I'll rip his arms from their sockets and beat him with them if I get to him again.

The blood in my veins churn from a simmer to a full boil. I jump to my feet, needing to work off the pent-up anger. My hands scrub my face as I stalk around the den of my mansion. Jagger forced me in here since the room doesn't have windows I can go through to escape.

Again, he was right since chaos still reigns in my mind. Thoughts of getting my hands on that fucker, pissed since I lost control, and my wolf howls incessantly.

I rub the ache in my chest.

Wren.

I need my fated mate.

But Jagger refuses to let me go to her until I calm down and regain control. He told me she witnessed the beginnings of my shift. Confusion filled her face. She tried to get to me. But he used his Alpha command to compel her to leave.

When Jagger told me she went home in the care of another male wolf shifter, my blood pressure skyrocketed. I stormed towards the door. He forced me back and told me that's why he couldn't let me see her yet. I had to get a grip.

Instead, he sent Sage to stay with my fated mate. Once again, our Luna prevented a catastrophe of epic portions. If humans learn of wolf shifters in Miami, they will hunt us down, then go in search of others. It would endanger beings besides wolf shifters. The secret existence of the paranormal world would end. And it would be all my fault.

Fortunately, the incident took place in the hallway with fewer people present. Sage cast spells to shroud the area and to stop time. Everyone froze. It didn't impact Jagger, our security team, or Wren. I blanked out when my wolf took over—again, a new happenstance. Jagger tells me he had to use his Alpha command to force the reversal of my shift. After Sage conjured clothes for me, a few of the security team brought me home.

Jagger stayed with Sage. She used her magick to repair the fucker's face and to erase everyone's memories of my attack before she released the other spells. He made me feel like an ass when he pointed out how she never wants to tamper with people's minds because of her and his experience years ago. I forced her hand. She used her teleportation magick to travel to Wren at The Larson Tower. Jagger came here with the rest of the team.

His ice blue eyes bore holes in my back as I stalk around, prowling like a caged animal. Tension swirls in the air. His disappointment in me proves palpable. As his beta, it's my responsibility to set an example for the rest of the pack members. For me to lose control in general is bad. But to beat a human male to a pulp then shift into my wolf all in public equates to a serious problem.

If only he and Sage witnessed my lapse in judgement, fine. However, our security team consists of pack enforcers. Not a good look for them to watch me go ballistic. Chances are they won't gossip since they don't commonly share what they do for the Alpha and beta. But the impression I made needs to be addressed. They're in the living room in case Jagger needs them. When I pull my mind from the brink, I'll speak with them.

Right now, I want my fated mate.

"Did Sage erase Wren's mind?"

Jagger blows a disgusted breath. He glares at me.

"*That's* your first question, Tag? You better be more concerned with your punishment than with Wren. She's fine. You are not."

For a minute I forget about him being my Alpha and glare back. Jagger doesn't miss my challenge.

He rises from the chair. Even though we're both six feet, seven inches and built like powerful Vikings, he draws on his Alpha traits to increase his stature. He appears taller and brawnier. His eyes darken to cobalt and flash with his silvery white wolf. The corners of his lips curl to reveal his elongated fangs. A low warning growl emanates from him. Fingernails lengthen to sharp claws. His Alpha command hits me in the chest like a sledgehammer.

I stagger back.

"Tag, you have been my best friend since we were pups. Do not go Dylan's route and challenge me when you know you shouldn't. Do you want years to pass before I allow you back in the pack? Think carefully on your answer."

I growl and whirl around. My fists punch holes in the wall. Plaster crumbles to the floor. Bones crack. Pain races up my arms. I howl more from the agony Wren may not accept me as a wolf shifter than from the ache coursing through me.

And here I worried I'd muck it up between us because I said something wrong. No, I just let her witness me beating her ex and shifting into a wolf.

The gods aren't crazy. I am.

WREN

"HI, MAY I COME IN?"

I nod as I open the doors wider for Sage to enter the duplex. The concierge surprised me when he rang the intercom to tell me she was downstairs. I hoped Tag would be with her. Disappointment washes over me when I don't see him.

Half an hour passed since I left the gala. Too upset to think straight, I left my gown on. My mind still can't make sense of the whole scenario. How badly Tag beat Jonathan. A relentless machine punching again and again. And the sound of Jonathan's bones breaking. I don't even want to think about it.

I shiver and wrap my arms around my torso as I close the double doors. Sage scans my face as she waits for me to get it together. I gesture towards the living room. She follows me and sits on the sofa. She has on her gown. So, I guess she came here directly. I lower myself on the other end, then hop up remembering my manners.

"Would you care for a drink?"

Sage nods.

"That fiasco calls for the bottle," she says with a wry smile.

"Yeah. What do you prefer? Tag has—"

My voice catches as I say his name aloud. I drop onto the sofa with a ragged sob. Arms wrap around me.

"Oh, honey. I know it's upsetting. Jagger is with Tag at his mansion on Moon Island. Don't worry, he's fine."

I blubber harder.

What the hell happened to my teddy bear? He turned into more than the beast the office staff dreads. An uncontrollable wild monster emerged and went on a rampage. His eyes flashed and his facial features morphed into what appeared to be a wolf.

But that just can't be!

I must be mistaken, which is why I tried to get to him. But Blake prevented me. Dammit! Then I realize Sage may know something. I sit back from her embrace and stare into her eyes. I search their emerald green depths as I ask her about Tag.

"You said he's fine. But I thought I saw his face change. I —I mean… somehow his features shifted. I've seen his eyes flash. But this time it was different. It was as though another force was behind them."

I pause and shake my head. My words sound crazy to

me. How must they sound to Sage? She must think I've lost it. I peek at her to gauge her reaction.

She stares back without a change in her expression. I'd have thought she would show surprise or tell me I was mistaken. Or bonkers. Weird.

"It must have been the lighting or… or… something. I—I don't know. But I want to talk to him. I *need* to talk to him. He's not answering his mobile. Will you call Jagger so I can speak to Tag?"

I rub the ache in my chest. Something feels so very wrong. Instinct tells me Tag can fix it. Even if my mind tells me he's a madman, and I need to stay away from him.

Sage stares at me a moment, then places her clutch on the coffee table next to my open sketchpad. Her hands pause as she opens the handbag. They reach for the sketchpad. Slowly, she turns the pages.

"Did you draw these pictures?"

I nod and shrug.

"Yes," I answer as I stare at the fantastical creatures on the pages.

She pauses on one where a male and a female wolf romp with three pups amongst pine trees near a marsh. It's the most recent sketch. Where I used to draw a variety, now wolves dominate my thoughts—and my dreams. Wolves!

"Sage, I really need to see Tag. I know where Moon Island is but not his mansion. Can you take me to him?"

"Why don't you go change while I call Jagger?"

My heart leaps as I rush from the living room. Less than

ten minutes later, I return to find Sage waiting in the entry foyer. We leave and head to the garage for my car. The ride doesn't take long. We turn off the causeway and pull up to intricate wrought-iron gates—the entrance to Moon Island. Two members of the security team sit in a guardhouse. Sage leans over from the passenger side to wave at them through the window. They recognize her and wave as the gates open.

She directs me towards Tag's home. As we drive along the main road, I admire the posh residences ranging from ranch style to two- and three-story. Some front Biscayne Bay, while others have interior views. We pull into the driveway of a grand Mediterranean Revival style mansion on the bay.

The glass and metalwork double doors open. Tag rushes out, followed by Jagger. The car barely stops before Tag opens my door. I put the car in park as he unfastens my seatbelt. He groans as he swoops me from the seat and buries his face in my hair. His heart slams in his chest. The familiar rumble wraps around me as he strides back inside.

I notice nothing or anyone. My arms tighten around his neck. I meld my body as close to his as possible. I inhale his intoxicating cologne mixed with his natural masculine scent. My body responds with need. The urge to make love to him overrides all else.

"Tag," I moan.

"I've got you, My Sweet Girl," he croons, and I melt.

"Tag, don't fuck up. I'm dead serious."

I lift my head, having forgotten about Jagger and Sage.

He narrows his eyes at Tag, who grunts in acknowledgment. Sage whispers in Jagger's ear and takes his arm to usher him out the door. I drop my head back on Tag's shoulder.

He climbs the stairs three at a time and jogs down the hall with ease. We enter the primary bedroom suite. He lowers me to my feet as my body slides along his. An arm bands around my waist while a hand cups my butt. He presses me close. My breasts flatten against his chest as our pelvises grind.

"I love you so much, Wren."

"Oh, Tag. I love you so much too!"

He growls and slams his mouth on mine. Once again, he sounds like a wild wolf. But I don't care. The ravenous kiss obliterates my mind. His demanding tongue pushes past my teeth and sweeps through my mouth. He tastes and conquers me all at once.

Toes curl in my flats as fingers tug his hair. I mewl as he ends the searing kiss with nips, licks, and sucks down the column of my throat to my shoulder. I shiver when he rakes his teeth against the sensitive flesh.

"Tell me you belong to me, Wren. Tell me you'll be mine forever."

My fingernails dig into his shoulders through the thin cotton of his t-shirt. I arch up into him, trying to seal us together. I want nothing between us. I need him more than imaginable.

"Yes, Tag. YES!"

He growls and lifts my maxi dress over my head. He

rips my simple cotton bra and matching G-string from my body. The gusset catches my clit, and I gasp. He drops to his knees, parts my slick folds, and kisses the engorged nubbin. The flat of his tongue laves my pussy from clit to slit. I dance on my toes as he eats me out with savage growls.

Before my knees collapse, he scoops me up and carries me to the king-size bed. He sets me on the edge and stands between my thighs. With his eyes on mine, he yanks his t-shirt off. I pull the drawstring of his sweatpants and push them from his narrow hips. His erect cock pops free. I lean forward and press my lips to the swollen tip. My tongue darts out to lap at the bead of pre-cum. I moan at his salty taste.

He groans.

"Need. You. Now."

He crawls over me as I scoot backwards to the center of the bed. His eyes, then mouth fasten on my bobbing breasts. I fall back to my elbows and moan as he suckles the plump nipples. He reaches between us and lines his cock with my core. A snap of his hips plunges him inside to the root. I whine at the instant stretch. He rumbles and places open-mouthed kisses in the hollow between my breasts, then up to my mouth open on a throaty moan.

He wraps his arms around me as he rocks in and out of my core. I wrap my thighs around his hips. My softness molds to the hard planes of his big body—a perfect fit.

We continue to move as one locked in a passionate embrace. I cry out as orgasms ripple through my pussy. Tag groans as my inner walls clench around his massive girth. He shifts the angle of penetration. The adjustment causes the tip of his cock to drag along my clit and against my G-spot.

I writhe beneath him as another orgasm builds. It starts from my toes to crackle up my legs until it explodes in my core. Legs stiffen and toes curl. My fingernails leave crescent moons as I cling to Tag's back. A garbled cry tumbles from between my parted lips. Eyes squeeze shut as the aftershocks roll through me.

My pleasure triggers his release. He rises to his knees and pulls my legs over his shoulders. His hands drop to the bed above my shoulders. Arms bracketing me in place. He stares down at me with eyes full of feral dominance and desire. Then his hips surge forward. Powerful thrusts drill me into the mattress.

I slide up. But his arms prevent me from moving too far. I grab them to ground myself. My breasts bounce with each pistoning thrust. Bent in half, my knees reach my ears. His big body dominates mine.

"MINE! Mine! Forever!

I scream in carnal rapture as a spine-tingling orgasm detonates.

Tag curses as his cock swells deep within me and copious amounts of his seed fill my womb. I pass out from the intensity.

I awake to Tag cleaning me with a warm, damp washcloth. I reach up and cup his cheek. He turns his head and kisses my palm, then looks at me. I frown at the worry in his eyes.

"You trust me, right?"

I nod, then answer, "Absolutely."

"I have something important to tell you."

He closes his eyes and takes a deep breath.

CHAPTER 14

Wren's mood switches from sexual bliss to worry as she stares at me with soulful eyes. I worry too. How the hell do I tell a human I'm a wolf shifter *and* she's my fated mate? The concept of a paranormal being alone will cause her to doubt me. Add to it our connection? Then the claiming bite and her transition?

I blow a breath and close my eyes to gather my words. I open them and take her hands in mine, praying to the gods she won't run from the house screaming.

"Let me tell you about how I got here."

She raises her eyebrows but doesn't ask the question.

I go on to tell her about our Viking origins and arrival

here, leaving the part about being wolf shifters out for now. She nods when I finish and smiles.

"That's all? After I saw your face at the gala, I thought you were going to tell me you're a werewolf! I knew I was hallucinating. Too many paranormal romance novels have me imagining things."

She giggles and squeezes my hands.

What the hell are paranormal romance novels?

But she's not far off. I'm paranormal, and we love each other. At least, I hope she still loves me after I tell her the rest.

"Wren, I'm not a werewolf. They're bloodthirsty and murderous creatures who can't control themselves."

As I say the words, I realize they describe my recent behavior. Well, damn. I shake my head, knowing that lapse was an anomaly. Completely uncharacteristic of me.

"I'm a shapeshifter. The kind that can shift from a man into a wolf at my will."

She stares at me.

I fight the urge to pull her onto my lap and snuggle into her to pretend as though I said nothing. But I have to be honest. I wait for her to speak.

"You're not joking, are you?"

"No."

She pulls her hands. I refuse to let her go and hold on tighter. My eyes implore her to stay. I want to issue the command she does not move, appealing to her submissive behavior. But it's more important she asks questions or tells me her thoughts. I get my wish. But not the words I hoped for.

"You're a monster! Let me go! Get off me!"

Her cries wound my heart and soul. My wolf howls in despair. I wrap my arms around her hips and lift her onto my lap. She pummels my chest with her fists. Her body shakes.

"You probably killed Jonathan! Oh my, God! I've had sex with a monster! No!!! Let. Me. Go!"

She slaps my face.

I don't stop her. I deserve her anger. Besides, my enhanced healing repairs any damage to my body within minutes. Her scant hits do nothing. Her words inflict damage. I tell myself she's just saying all those things because she's upset. She can't possibly mean them, especially after she told me she loves me and we made love. I won't let her take that away from me—from us.

"Wren, listen to me. I know you're upset—"

"Upset?!" She shrills. "You think I'm upset?! I'm beyond upset, Tag! You lied to me! Knowing you're a wolf shifter and didn't tell me. You let me fall in love with you. You're as bad as Jonathan! Both liars! I hate you, Tag! I hate you..."

Her words trail off as she sobs. Tears spill from her eyes. They slide down her reddened cheeks and drip on her heaving breasts. She stops hitting me and covers her face with both hands. Her body trembles.

My heart breaks.

However, she's right. I lied to her by omission. But at the same time, how could I tell her—a human—about my true nature? Look at how she reacts now, even after admitting she trusts and loves me. If I told her sooner, who knows what she would've done?

I have to get her to accept me. If not, Jagger says he'll ask Sage to wipe her and Maya's minds of me completely and move her back to Maya's condo while they were in a resting state. It would be as though Wren never knew me. And I cannot have that happen. She's my fated mate. She's mine.

"Wren, baby, please listen to me," I plead as I rock her in my arms and rumble. "Look at it from my perspective. No humans—other than those who are mated to shifters—know of our existence. Since time immemorial, our kind has lived alongside humans and survived because we keep our abilities a secret. Think of what would happen if scientists learned of our existence. They would capture us and conduct experiments. We would die."

I pause to let her absorb the impact.

She stops squirming but remains tense. I take it as a good sign.

"Now, think of how I've been with you. You admit you trust me. You say you fell in love with me—as I have with you. Have I done anything other than respect you, care for you, protect you?"

She shakes her head, then opens her mouth.

I know what she's about to say and speak first.

"Yes, I beat that fucker. And I'd do it again. You know why?"

She shakes her head. I cock an eyebrow.

"No."

"Because he hurt you. He put his hands on you against your will and yanked you so hard you cried out. I will allow no one to hurt you. Didn't I tell you that earlier about your uncle and aunt?"

"Yes."

"Do you know how I knew from all the way across the ballroom?"

"No."

I place my hand over her heart and her hand over mine.

She raises her eyes to my face.

"You feel the connection we share, don't you? That sense of the other's presence and emotions?" When she agrees, I continue. "That's called the mate bond."

Her eyes widen.

"Y—You called me mate before."

"Yes."

"In my PNR novels, that's the same as marriage between humans. You feel it with me?"

"Yes. Even more so since you, Wren Byrd, are my fated mate. Do your books explain the meaning?"

Her jaw drops. I use the tip of my index finger to close it. She nods her head.

"Are you telling me you and I are fated to be together by the gods? Oh, my God! You always say, 'the gods!' I assumed you misspoke. The more I think about it, you act like the Alpha heroes in my novels. But that's fiction! This is real life, Tag! I—I need proof."

I figured she'd ask. I slide her onto the bed and rise.

"Remember, even in wolf form, I'm still me, Tag. I love you and will never harm you. Don't be frightened. Do you understand?"

"Yes," she whispers as she sits up and stares at me intensely.

My body relaxes. This time, I allow my wolf to take over, not giving him full control like earlier. Ordinarily, my other half lives on the fringes of my being. Always ready to spring forth at my command, then retreat at my will. An ability born of our kind so long ago and marks us different from full humans.

The sensations of my bones reshaping and muscles lengthening to shift me from my human form to that of my great sable brown wolf block out my fated mate on the bed. Crackling and a flash find me on all four massive paws within moments.

I swivel my enormous head to pin her with my flashing gaze.

Her mouth gapes as she stares, enthralled. Curious eyes take me in from my snout to the tip of my feathery tail. Every inch of my body thrums from the intensity of her stare. Frissons of electricity roll through me.

The desire to go to her, rub my body on hers, and cover her in my scent proves hard to resist. But I will. My fated mate has to come to me. Accept me and my wolf. I sit on my haunches and wait.

"C—Can you understand me?"

My head nods as my eyes remain fixed on hers.

She gnaws the corner of her bottom lip. I want to suck

it into my mouth. A few minutes pass before she scoots across the bed. She picks up my t-shirt and slips it over her head. A toothy grin spreads on my face seeing her in my clothes. She's well over a foot shorter than me. The hem reaches above her knees barely.

She pauses and gasps.

I cock my head, then realize my teeth. Duh! I close my mouth. On further thought, I lower my belly to the floor with my snout between my front paws in a less threatening posture.

My fated mate approaches me with measured steps. I don't move. Hell, I don't even breathe.

"So, you understand me. Can you talk?"

I whine in the back of my throat and glance up at her.

She nods.

"Can I touch you?"

I yip and thump my tail on the floor.

She smiles and kneels in front of me. Tentatively, she extends her hand. Again, I hold my breath and stare at her with pleading eyes. When her small hand lands between my ears, I close my eyes and sigh. Her touch calms me. I rumble in my chest.

"Oh, you like that huh?" She asks as her palm smooths my fur. "I cannot believe I'm actually petting a wolf shifter. Talk about a vivid imagination. Wow."

I want to bristle at the petting reference. Wolf shifters are not dogs. But I let it go. My fated mate is smiling. That's what matters—not my ego. I yip and press my head up into her hand.

She leans on her other hand and crawls further along my body to touch my flanks and back.

The all-fours position makes my cock thicken wedged between my belly and the floor. How I want to mount her on her hands and knees and issue the claiming bite. I close my eyes and will myself to stay in control.

"You're much bigger than regular wolves."

In every way, baby.

She continues to murmur her findings as I lie still. Finally, she makes her way around my entire body. She sits with her legs tucked to the side.

Daring to touch her, I crawl forward and place my head on her lap. She startles at the size compared to her small lap. I nuzzle against her rumbling in my chest. She places her hand on my neck and pats me. I close my eyes and inhale her unique scent mixed with our combined sex. Never a better aroma existed.

Both lost in thought, we sit in silence.

Then my mobile rings. I growl. My fated mate yelps and scoots away. Damn.

In a blink, I shift back. I cup her cheek and smile.

"Sorry, baby. I didn't mean to startle you. I just hate my mobile disturbed us. Give me a minute. It's probably Jagger checking on you."

I jump to my feet and snatch the mobile from my sweatpants pocket. Yup, Jagger.

"Yeah."

"What's going on?"

I glance over my shoulder at my fated mate. My t-shirt is halfway over her head. I frown.

"Wren, what are you doing?"

She bites her lower lip as her cheeks pinken. Then tosses the t-shirt to the bed and picks up her dress.

"I need to go."

My stomach drops. No! I can't let her leave. Not now, before we resolve everything. And I haven't told her about the transition.

"Jagger, listen, I gotta go."

"Tell me what's going on first."

I stalk over to Wren and take her hand. As I answer Jagger, I stare into her eyes, talking more to her than to him.

"I told Wren about being a wolf shifter. She trusts and loves me. I love her. That's what's most important. We need to finish our conversation. I have to go."

"Fine."

I end the call and toss my mobile on top of my sweats, then squeeze my fated mate's hand. I lead her back to the bed. She's hesitant. I turn and stroke her cheek. Her eyes close. I kiss the top of her head and scoop her into my arms, carrying her the rest of the way.

I sit with her straddling my lap and my back against the headboard. My body temperature runs high. But I want her comfortable in the air-conditioned bedroom. So, I tuck the sheets around us.

"Tag, I don't know what you want me to say," she starts

as she gazes at a spot over my shoulder. "It's a lot to digest. I don't know."

Taking her chin between my thumb and index finger, I bring her gaze to meet mine. I keep my expression open so she can see I'm being completely honest.

"Wren, I know it must sound absurd to you. But you saw me shift—"

"Wait a minute! Are Jagger and Sage wolf shifters too?" She shrieks, then her eyes widen. "Moon Island! Is everyone living here like you?!"

"Yes, to both."

She covers her eyes with one hand and shakes her head, mumbling to herself. My ears pick up parts of it. It can't be real. Unbelievable. Incredible. Can only happen to me. I let her talk it out while I rumble and stroke her back. Abruptly, she swats my hands away.

"Stop making that noise and touching me! I can't think straight when you do it!" She cries and pushes both palms against my chest. "I. Need. To. Go. Now."

I catch her hands and hold them to my heart.

"Wren, there's more."

She inhales sharply. Her eyes narrow on me.

"Like all male wolf shifters, when I was born, my first breath carried the scent of my fated mate—cinnamon sugar caramel apples. At a charity gala at the Larson Miami Hotel & Resort a few weeks ago, I caught the scent on the breeze. Were you there?"

She blinks in surprise and nods.

"I searched but couldn't find you. Three weeks later, I

caught your unique scent in the elevator. I smell it on you now, mixed with my signature. There is no doubt you are my fated mate, Wren. You may not understand. But it's true. And not every male finds his fated mate. It's rare. Something we cherish."

I search her face, willing her to accept me. She doesn't fight me. So, I continue.

"Most wolf shifters mate within our kind. Sometimes a male wolf shifter and a human female fall in love. Our pack has had a few such pairings. The last being at least thirty years ago. Perhaps your books have occurrences?"

She breathes a yes.

"When our kind mate, the male issues a claiming bite, here," I say and skim the juncture of her neck and shoulder with my fingertip. She shivers, then her eyes pop.

"Of course! That's why you always lick and nip me there."

Now, I nod.

"I've wanted to claim you from the first moment your scent filled my nostrils and every time thereafter. But I controlled myself and my wolf, who knows you're ours.

"Not only will it be a claiming bite for you where a serum lodges my scent in your skin permanently. But it will enact the transformation of you into a wolf shifter. I'll be in human form, and the serum will drip from my extended canines. I will gift you with the ability to be one with me in every way.

"It involves the risk your body won't accept the transformation. You may take it completely and shift. Or not, and only benefit from our longer life spans and enhanced abilities. Since we're fated mates and based on past wolf shifter-human fated mate bondings, you will be fine.

"However, the choice is yours. I will not force you. I love you and want us to have a family and spend the rest of our lives together."

Tears fill her eyes.

I lean forward and kiss her lips softly. My forehead presses to hers, and I inhale her breath.

She leans back.

"Well, since we're being honest, I have to admit PNR isn't my first fascination with fantastical creatures. As a child, I read fairy tales and fell in love with that world. They helped me to escape from a sad reality. Now, I enjoy the spicier side of that world with my romance novels."

She pauses as her cheeks flush.

"I've had constant dreams about you and wolves for weeks now. I thought it was just my imagination running wild with my books. Then my drawings changed from wolves, witches, fairies, vampires, and other what I thought were fantastical creatures to only wolves. Sage saw my sketchpad earlier and asked me about it."

Now, my mouth drops. My fated mate closes it with a slight smile.

"But I still need time to think about all you've told me, Tag. It's a lot to accept. You must understand," she says, then arches an eyebrow. "From my perspective."

"Touché," I nod in acknowledgment of her using my words back at me.

She smiles and climbs from my lap. I catch her hand.

"Wait. Where are you going?"

She frowns and responds, "Home. I need space to think, Tag."

I shake my head.

"I can't let you leave Moon Island, Wren."

 ren

"I WANT you to stay here with me in our home. Otherwise, you will stay with Jagger and Sage next door."

My mouth gapes, then I sputter in shock.

"You have to be kidding me, Tag. I can't stay here surrounded by wolf shifters. I'd be scared to death!"

He cocks his head as his lips flatten.

"You do realize you've been 'surrounded by wolf shifters' for weeks now?"

I frown, thinking I've only interacted with Jagger a few times in passing and Sage tonight. What is he talking about?

"Well, let's see. Beth, Ginny, Dana. Remember them?

How about pretty much seventy percent of Larson Enterprises' staff?"

My mouth drops. The way I'm going tonight, I might as well turn into a fish. But how the hell didn't I realize they were wolf shifters or she-wolves or whatever?!

Then, as I think about it, I recall the way Beth's nostrils flared slightly or how her gaze could be so piercing, like a predator. The stealth-like movements of the security team. So many nuances I didn't pay attention to. Just like Tag said, they walk amongst us undetected. No one thinks any differently about them. One would have to know what to look for in order to tell them apart from regular humans. Amazing.

"Were you 'scared to death' being in close proximity to us?"

I have to admit I wasn't. At. All.

They treated me no differently than any full human.

"No."

"And do you truly believe I would allow anyone—human or otherwise—to harm you?"

My heart tells me absolutely not. However, my brain still sticks on their numbers.

It shocks me to know there are so many of them. Larson Enterprises is an enormous company. This island has dozens of residences. Another revelation hits me.

"Besides Miami, are there others?"

"Yes."

"A lot?" I ask tremulously, visualizing millions of wolf shifters around the world.

"Yes."

Another thought occurs to me.

"You said you're a shifter who can turn into a wolf. Does that mean there are *other* kinds of shifters?"

"Yes."

My mind goes back to the fairy tales. I've always wondered if the different creatures and their stories held a bit of truth. People speak of and write what they know. It may not make sense to me. But I'm not arrogant enough to dispel the possibilities completely. I just never thought they'd be true to this extent. I mean, Tag is a wolf shifter and I'm his fated mate? What???

It's too much to wrap my head around now. It's late. I've had enough with the drama and the emotional roller-coaster. My brain needs to shut off. I wish I could reboot the whole damn day!

Tag must sense my anxiety. The rumble reaches my ears as loving warmth touches my heart. He squeezes my hand and watches me with soft eyes.

I'm oh so tempted to fall into his arms, bury my face in his chest, and fall asleep. But I do need space. He's too much. My thoughts jumble in his presence. I just can't believe he refuses to let me leave. What the hell?!

"Tag, I need to sleep and not here. I don't want to stay with Sage and Jagger. I want to go home, get into my bed, and close my eyes. Why is that a problem?"

The corners of his mouth droop. Pain flashes in his eyes.

"We can't risk anyone finding out about us, Wren. And

before you say it, I trust you. But a slip-up can happen. Look at what happened to me the night of the charity gala, and I need to guard our secret with my life."

I growl in frustration and yank my hand from his grip. I march in a circle, waving my arms in the air.

"What the hell does that mean? How long do I remain captive? What about work? When do I see Maya? What about my life?!"

I spin around and glare at him. I'm tired and frustrated. If I seem like a petulant child, so be it.

He rises from the bed with that predatory grace I should have recognized before and do now. Sorrow mars his handsome face.

My heart clenches. I rub at the ache in my chest where our mate bond floods with his emotions. My sadness blends with his. I hate we feel this way. I miss the warmth. How can we get back to before? Is it even possible? Do I really want to?

"Wren, I can't say that I wish things were completely different. If that were the case, you wouldn't be my fated mate," Tag says as he strides towards me. He shakes his head. "I will say my life plan didn't include a relationship now. Work and pack were all that mattered to me. And as you know, I lead a highly structured life. It brooks no room for unexpected situations."

His fingertips brush against my cheek as a gentle smile lifts the corners of his mouth. Warmth seeps through the mate bond. My heart flutters.

"Then you came into my life like a whirlwind," he says

and chuckles. "Hiding from me. The elevator getting stuck out of the blue. A distraction at work. Gossip amongst the pack. A fight where I shift in front of humans. On top of it all, my wolf going feral, eager to claim you. I lost control for the first time in my life."

He shakes his head as his smile widens.

"You made me realize having you as my fated mate supplants all else. I want us to be together. Badly. I don't want to stop your life. I want to be a part of it," he says, then smirks. "Well, the largest part, of course."

I sigh in relief.

"If you truly trust and love me, then give me the chance. No. Give *us* a chance. I'll even take time off from work. We'll go to the Everglades. Our pack has a camp there where fewer members live. We'll stay in my cabin. You can experience life with me and the pack with the knowledge of our kind. Everyone will welcome you and answer all questions you have. If after a month you choose to walk away, I will not stop you. Do you agree?"

I stare up into his emerald green depths. Hope shines within them. How can I dim that light when I want to walk in its warmth forever?

"Yes."

A smile bursts across his face as he whoops and lifts me from the floor. He spins around, then lowers me to my feet. His mouth covers mine for a tender kiss. He brushes his lips against mine, then stares at me fiercely.

"I love you, Wren Byrd and vow to make you accept us before the month ends."

"MY PARENTS TOOK me to the Everglades when I was around five. We rode on an airboat. I remember how green the area was and the alligators slithering in the water. They scared me. But my parents held me between them. They told me the gators can't get me, but I could eat them. After the ride, we ate fried alligator strips. Not my favorite."

I laugh, and Tag joins in.

We're flying above the marshland in his spacious luxury helicopter.

Before we left Miami, I called Maya to let her know I was going on a trip with Tag for a few weeks. She clapped gleefully. We stopped by my condo for me to change and to pack. I brought my sketchpad and my laptop, even though Tag says we won't work. I have some open activities I can't neglect. Besides, I saw his laptop case. He's too much of a stickler to leave his responsibilities unattended. I don't mind.

A knock on the door separating the cabin from the crew area and cockpit draws my attention from the window. Tag calls for them to enter.

"We land in fifteen minutes, beta. Would you care for anything before?" The flight attendant asks.

Tag introduced me to the crew as his fated mate. Just as he predicted, they greeted me pleasantly. Once we were airborne, he told me they're members of the pack. The flight attendant is a young she-wolf mated to the pilot. The co-pilot is an unmated older male.

Tag smiled when I told him I recognize the term beta from my PNR novels. He gave me more details about his role and that of the beta's mate. My heart swells each time he teaches me more about wolf shifters and his pack. Including their official name—Miami Wolves Pack.

I told him their nickname of *Billionaire Wolves of Miami* was apropos given Larson Enterprises' holdings, Moon Island, and his helicopter. I laughed when he told me about his private jet and *Moonbeam*—Jagger's 465-foot megayacht the members have access to. Yeah, they're an über-wealthy pack.

Tag glances at me with a raised eyebrow. I smile at the flight attendant and decline. We ate a decadent breakfast of eggs royale with caviar and Maltaise sauce during the flight. Yum! So, I'm nice and full.

He declines too, and the flight attendant leaves us. Tag takes my hand and brings it to his lips. He brushes them over my knuckles.

"Ready?" He murmurs as his eyes stare up at me. The bright sunlight makes them sparkle like emeralds.

I pause to think about it. Would I ever imagine I'd be about to spend a month in the Everglades as the only human amongst wolf shifters I never knew existed? Ah… That would be a firm no. However, as George always told me, I have a vivid imagination. If I can swoon over an Alpha carrying his mate to ravish her in my novels, why can't I experience it in real life with my fated mate?

"Yes!"

Tag's eyes spark. He cups the back of my head and

kisses me senseless. I swoon against him with a contented sigh. If he keeps this up, he'll have me convinced in no time.

The helicopter lands in a clearing. We thank the crew. Tag helps me out and grabs our bags. He leads me to a Range Rover where a male wolf shifter stands. He raises his hand as we approach.

"Greetings, beta!"

"Ulf, good to see you!" Tag responds, then turns to me. "Wren, this is Ulf. He's in charge of our Everglades property. Ulf, meet my fated mate, Wren Byrd."

He extends his hand with a broad smile.

"Welcome, Wren! Nice to meet you. If you need anything, my mate and I, along with the others, are here for you."

"Thank you so much, Ulf. How kind of you," I respond with a smile, shaking his hand.

He takes the bags from Tag and loads them in the SUV. Tag helps me in the backseat, then settles in the passenger seat. Ulf hops in, and we drive off.

Tag gives another lesson about the pack's camp.

It's the place they go for pack runs and trainings. For generations, the virtually untouched area of the subtropical wilderness allows them the freedom to be in their wolf form without prying eyes. Over the years, the original pack grounds grew from temporary cloth shelters to simple wooden cabins and now to luxurious residences scattered around the Alpha's house and clubhouse. Glamping—or glamorous camping—as Signy, Jagger's younger sister calls it.

Tag explains how a few families and security members known as enforcers choose to remain here, not wanting the hustle and bustle of Miami for their principal home.

I don't blame them. On days like this one with low humidity, a clear blue sky with the sun shining above, and clean air to fill your lungs, who wouldn't want to be here?

As we drive towards the camp, Tag and Ulf point out spots of interest. They share stories about various escapades over the years. I giggle as Tag recalls how Viggo and Rust—Jagger's younger brother and the pack doctor— snatched eggs from an alligator's nest and she chased them up a tree.

Soon, we round a bend. The pine trees open up to reveal the camp. It sprawls out before us. Rather, the glamp since every cabin is a rustic mansion of logs and stones in various styles—some ranch and others multilevel, with and without front porches. They surround an open park-like square in the middle, where a lovely garden displays colorful flowers and bushes with wooden benches. Lanes crisscross the land to provide access to the various homes and structures.

A few pack members walk along or sit on porches. Their laughter and conversations fill the air. Cheerful smiles spread across their faces as they interact. The only surprising difference being some members in wolf form going about their business like it's an ordinary occurrence.

Otherwise, the camp is an idyllic enclave with the spectacular Everglades as the setting.

Ulf pulls up to a two-story mansion-size log cabin with a wraparound porch. Red flowers in window boxes add vibrant color to its wooden facade. Double doors hand carved with the face of a wolf gazing at the center square as though watching over the camp. The wolf reminds me of Tag's role as pack beta to care for them.

"This is us, babe. The one on the left is Jagger and Sage's cabin," Tag says, pointing beyond the windshield.

"If you call ritzy mansions cabins!" I laugh and hop out of the SUV. "I guess like the cottages of Newport, huh?"

The guys laugh as they climb out. Ulf gets the bags while Tag sweeps me from my feet. He carries me to the doors. I turn the knobs, and he strides inside.

"Welcome to our Everglades home, my fated mate."

I glance around at the double-height great room filled with comfortable leather furniture and a massive stone wall with an oversized fireplace. A wall of windows brings the scenery inside. The back porch expands to a deck to accommodate multiple seating areas and a swanky outdoor kitchen. An eat-in chef's kitchen and dining area finish the space. It reminds me of a layout in *Architectural Digest*.

"It's gorgeous, Tag," I breathe, awed by the home.

He grins and sets me on my feet, then takes my hand.

"Time for a tour."

Besides the great room, the home features a guest bathroom, media room, and den on the main level. Spacious four bedroom suites with attached baths take up the second level. The primary bedroom suite has a double-sided iron and glass fireplace between the sitting room and the bedroom.

Tag flips a switch, and the fireplace roars to life. He turns to me with a feral gleam in his darkened eyes. He scoops me up and carries me to the giant, hand-carved, four-poster wooden bed.

"Time to welcome you fully, my fated mate."

ag

"I BET we'll beat you guys!"

Wren yells as the 600-plus horsepower engines of the airboats rev to life. She adjusts the noise-canceling headset and puts on goggles.

Ulf chuckles as she gives him two thumbs up. He glances at me for approval, and I nod. Even though my wolf is none too pleased my fated mate is in his boat and not mine. But it was her idea to race me through the sawgrass marshes. And whatever makes her happy, I'm willing to do.

Just as I have these last two weeks.

Every question she asks I or a pack member answer. We go on hikes with me in human and wolf form. My wolf loves it when he gets a chance to interact with our fated mate. He doesn't even mind her scratching between our ears while making baby talk. Soon he'll let her put a collar and a leash on us. She enjoys group mealtimes where we gather in the dining hall to eat as a pack for breakfast or dinner. It's one way we keep our communal bond strong. Ulf's mate and several other she-wolves make certain to include Wren in activities where she may learn more about our lives. They garden, collect herbs and plants, and babysit the young pups. I indulge whatever keeps a smile on her face.

So, I smile and give her the thumbs up. She claps her hands, then grips the metal handrail. A pack member on the shore waves a flag. The airboats zip ahead. My fated mate's shouts make my wolf panic. But he calms at her laughter. I shake my head.

We race through open channels, skimming across the shallow waters. Coastal mangroves rise from roots that resemble legs. Beneath them, leatherback turtles and West Indian manatees forage for food. A pair of bald eagles soar above, calling to one another with high-pitch whistles. Near the shoreline, a great egret stands as still as a statue, waiting to snag its next meal.

A brilliant sun shines on my fated mate's excited face as she points at the sights. The wind whips tendrils loose from her long braid. The sun glints off the rich mahogany brown strands.

I recall the many times I wound her hair around my fist as I pounded her pussy from behind. The erotic recollections make my cock twitch. I shift on the bench and shake my head.

We turn a corner and the pack member navigating my airboat taps my shoulder. I follow the direction his finger points. Up ahead, alligators churn the water in a feeding frenzy. Their death rolls as they tear apart their prey disturb the peaceful scene.

Our airboats slow down.

"Listen, give them a wide berth. Ulf, you guys go first. We'll follow. Do not go near those gators," I command into the headset's built-in radio. "Wren, hold on tight. Do not move."

"Yes, beta."

"Yes, beta."

"Yes, Tag."

Her bright smile disappears as she eyes the predators warily. A couple of white-tailed deer made the fatal mistake of getting too close to the water's edge. The alligators lurk beneath the surface. They grab prey before they even know what happened. My poor fated mate doesn't understand the ways of predators. She'll have to learn.

Once we pass the voracious gators, the airboats resume their speed. Relieved, my fated mate turns and gives me the thumbs up. I return the gesture with a broad smile. She's happy again. All is well.

We return to the camp's docks from a different direction. I jump off the airboat and help my fated mate. She grins at me and wraps her arms around my neck. I hold her around the waist and swing her around. She throws her head back and laughs.

The sight of her bare neck and shoulder makes my wolf howl. We want to claim her sooner rather than later. But I'm a patient male. She's almost ready.

"That was so much fun!" She exclaims as I set her on her feet. Then she frowns. "Well, except for those alligators. They frightened me. So many in one spot. That poor animal. They ripped it apart."

I take her hand and lead her to the SUV.

"It's the way of nature, babe. And they caught two white-tailed deer."

Her frown deepens.

"That's even worse."

I open the passenger-side door and lift her onto the seat, then shut the door. I round the front and sit behind the wheel. Taking her hand in mine, I squeeze it.

"Wren, predators eat prey. It's the circle of life. Wolf shifters are apex predators. We hunt and eat animals."

She chews on the corner of her lower lip as she considers my words. I wait until she speaks. Her eyes avoid mine.

"Does that mean I would have to hunt and eat innocent animals if I transition?"

"Yes. But remember, it's instinct for a predator to do so. Once you transition, your wolf will want to hunt. You will learn to enjoy the thrill of the chase and the satisfaction of your meal. Don't you enjoy a good steak?"

I smirk as her eyes narrow. She huffs and yanks her hand from mine.

"Whatever. Drive, Tag."

I chuckle wickedly and poke her side. She squeals, slapping at my hand. I keep tickling her until the smile returns on her face.

"But I don't eat my steak *raw!*" She quips once she catches her breath.

"Pity. It's oh so delicious, my fated mate," I say as I smack my lips.

She growls and rolls her eyes, plopping back in the seat, arms folded across her chest. But the corners of her mouth curl up in a smile as she stares out the window.

I place a possessive hand on her thigh and drive. When she doesn't swat it away, I smirk. Another win.

She relaxes as we drive along the road to camp.

My mobile rings. I answer it through the SUV's system. Jagger's voice fills the interior.

"How's it going?"

I glance at Wren. She smiles.

"You're on speaker. My fated mate can answer," I respond with a wink at her.

"Hi, Jagger. Thank you for asking. Everything is great! The pack welcomes me and treats me no differently than anyone else. You have a gorgeous camp. Such a lovely retreat from Miami. I love it here."

"That's great to hear, Wren—"

"Indeed, it is! And Tag treats you well, too, I guess?" Sage asks cutting in with a giggle.

My fated mate's cheeks flush as her eyes dart to mine. I smirk.

"Yes, you guess correctly," she responds.

"Excellent! We won't hold you. Call if you need anything," Jagger says as Sage voices her agreement.

"Thanks!" We reply in unison, then laugh as I end the call.

She shifts in the seat to face me.

"I like Sage and Jagger. It's really nice of them to check in on me."

I squeeze her thigh as I nod.

"Yes. And remember, as Alpha and Luna, the pack's happiness ranks high for them. One reason everyone respects them. They genuinely care for each member equally. As you've experienced, our pack is well balanced."

She lowers her eyes and nibbles on her lip.

"What's the matter?"

"But I'm not part of your pack."

Wren

For a second, Tag's eyes dim. Then he squeezes my thigh and grins.

"Not officially yet, my fated mate. That happens after I claim you, and we complete our mate bonding ceremony."

In Maya's words, he's *not just good. But really good.*

"We'll see, Tag Dahl."

He nods as his grin widens.

We continue on in companionable silence.

My thoughts move to the claiming bite and the transition. I asked a few of the mated she-wolves about the bite. They say it's done during sex at the point of orgasm. So, although it's painful—you know, sharp fangs puncturing flesh and all—it intensifies the pleasure of the orgasm. A hyped-up climax, they giggled.

My nipples pebbled, and my core clenched. It sounds incredible. However, that's not the part that worries me. It's the transition. They had little knowledge about it since they're born she-wolves. Like Tag already told me, they know decades ago was the last occurrence. But they told me the turned she-wolves would be happy to speak to me. However, they're in Miami on Moon Island.

I'm sure Tag would arrange for me to meet with them. To learn about their experiences would help me a lot. I glance over at him. Even though he keeps his eyes on the road, he smirks. I roll my eyes.

We reach the camp and park in the garage. Tag helps me from the SUV. I hold his hand as we walk to his cabin. Now's as good a time as any to ask about the turned she-wolves.

"I want to learn more about the transition," I start.

He peers down at me and nods.

"Ask away, babe."

I shake my head.

"The she-wolves I spoke to about it and the claiming

bite tell me the turned she-wolves would speak with me about their experiences. Will you arrange for me to meet them? Maybe when we get back?"

He tilts his head thoughtfully.

"How about I set up a video conference call? That way, you won't have to wait another two weeks."

"Perfect, thanks," I respond, happy he doesn't mind me asking more details. It's not that I don't trust him. But I want first-hand accounts.

He pulls out his mobile and makes calls as we continue to the cabin. By the time we get inside, he's scheduled the call in thirty minutes. I rush upstairs to shower. When I meet him in the den, he has the flat-screen television set for the call. He kisses the top of my head and leaves me to speak with the she-wolves in private. I smile at his thoughtfulness.

Moments later, the call connects. Three older she-wolves appear on screen. They greet me with warm smiles. I thank them for taking the time to speak with me. They wave me off, saying it's their pleasure.

"I'm not sure how much Tag told you. But I'll tell you a bit about me and where we are with our relationship."

They nod and voice words of encouragement. I give them a summary from the elevator to now. When I finish, I tell them my concerns about the transition. I also ask they share their experiences not just with the claiming but as humans adapting to being she-wolves.

Each one tells her story. Like me, they're fated mates. Prior to meeting their male wolf shifters, they never knew of the beings' existence. It happened where the males approached them after detecting their unique scents. Like Tag, they wooed the women without mentioning their true natures.

Two of the women fell in love with their fated mates right away. The third rejected hers initially. All admit they felt the attraction and later learned it's the mate bond. What changed the third she-wolf's mind was the persistence of her fated mate. He never gave up. Like Tag.

Once the women committed to the relationships, the males confessed. All three balked. But the solid foundation of love developed proved stronger than their fear, anger, and shock. They accepted their fated mates and decided to be one with them in all ways. The males claimed them.

Like the born she-wolves, the women felt pain and pleasure in the bite. They blush as they describe it to me. Heat rises in my cheeks too. I can't speak for their cores. But mine aches for Tag.

When they describe the transition, I perk up, not wanting to miss any detail. After the bite, they felt woozy and drifted in and out of sleep for a few days. They couldn't remember much more other than their fated mates never let their sides. The males fed them soft foods and liquids. Days later, they awoke invigorated, stronger than before.

Their wolves appeared on the fringes of their beings. The males taught the new she-wolves how to connect with their other half through their minds and to call them forward to shift. The women describe it as their bodies painlessly realigning to the shape of their wolves in moments. They remain in full control of their bodies and their minds. The world appears more vibrant.

They laugh at the increase in their sexual appetites. I giggle, thinking if mine grows anymore, I'll never get out of bed. As for the hunting, they agree with Tag—it's nature.

One woman didn't transition fully. But she lives longer with better health. The pack treats her equally.

They completed the mate bonding ceremony—the wolf shifter's version of a wedding ceremony—after their transition. Their eyes grow dreamy as they recall their special days. Each of them gave birth to healthy pups. They laugh when I ask if the babies came out human or wolf. Relief sweeps through me when they confirm human. I couldn't imagine giving birth to a four-legged miniature wolf!

Overall, they love their lives with their fated mates, family, and the pack. The women assure me pack life does not differ from human families. However, wolves remain loyal and dedicated to the wellbeing of all pack members. The hierarchy of Alpha, Luna, beta, enforcers, and down keep the pack in order. The Alpha and Luna are fair and loved by all.

The women laugh and tell me to ask Sage about her experience. They tell me it's even more extraordinary than theirs. I make a mental note to ask Tag if she would mind sharing.

By the end of the call, my nerves lessen. I'm eager to get to my fated mate. With many thanks and their well wishes, I end the call.

My body thrums with need of my fated mate. I rush from the den, checking the rooms I pass. In the great room, I glance out the wall of windows. My heart swells.

Tag stretches out on a chaise lounge sipping scotch.

I admire him for a moment. The late afternoon breeze ruffles his sable brown hair. He shaved the five o'clock shadow this morning since it grew to more of a beard these last two weeks. The dimple in his chin adds a softness to his strong jawline. A long-sleeve t-shirt covers his broad shoulders and sculpted torso. Low-slung joggers encase his long, muscular legs. They cross at the ankles as they extend to the very end of the chaise lounge.

My fated mate's masculine beauty and strength call to my feminine desires. My core softens as my juices flow, preparing for him to take me. Every cell in my body explodes with desire. I whine in the back of my throat as the pressure builds in my core. On weak knees, I cross the great room and slide the glass door open.

"I sense your need for me. Come, my fated mate."

He turns to me with eyes as smoky as his gruff voice.

A strangled, lust-filled cry slips past my lips as I rush to his side. He sets the crystal tumbler on a side table and opens his arms to me. I fall into them, straddling his thick thighs. My fingers dig into his shoulders as I stare into his eyes.

"Tag Dahl, I love you with every fiber of my being. Wholeheartedly, I accept you as a wolf shifter and as my fated mate. I wish to be with you forever and to bear your pups. I ask you to make me yours in all ways."

He responds with a low and husky growl as he leans forward and licks the juncture of my neck and shoulder.

My core clenches on an orgasm. I cry out in surprise as my fingernails dig into his shoulders. Another lusty growl and my core clenches again.

"Oh, Tag… I need you… inside me," I pant, grinding my pussy against his burgeoning erection. It bobs beneath me, and I moan, increasing my pace. A swift smack to my ass halts my movements. I cry out in half pain and half pleasure.

"I give you your pleasure, naughty girl," he chides in a raspy voice.

"Oh, please, Sir. Please!"

He grunts and lifts the hem of my sundress around my hips, exposing my bare pussy. Since we've been here, he doesn't allow me to wear panties. And in the cabin, I rarely wear any clothing.

I pull on the collar of his long-sleeve t-shirt, needing to feel his heated flesh beneath my palms, aching for skin-to-skin connection. He obliges and yanks it over his head. My eager fingers reach for the drawstring of his joggers. I tug it and pull on the waistband as my mouth waters at the outline of his long, thick cock. He raises his hips. The joggers lower to his thighs.

My fingers wrap around his shaft. It's so wide, the tips don't meet. I stroke up and squeeze the plum-shaped head. He groans as a bead of pre-cum leaks from the slit. I scoot back on his thighs and bend over to lap at the thick, milky seed.

His fingers grip my hair. He pushes my head down. I open my mouth. His cock slides along my tongue to the back of my throat. I gag, then relax with a hum. He groans and grinds his hips. I bob along his cock until it swells.

With a snarl, he pulls me up, fists his base, and glides his shaft along my dripping folds, coating it in my arousal. I moan, greedy for more. He doesn't make me wait. He aligns his cock with my entrance and thrusts up as he grips my hips firmly. Fast pistoning strokes bring us to climax quickly. Our bodies shake from the intensity. My passionate cries and his primal howl resound through the pine trees.

Birds take to the air, squawking their dissatisfaction at being disturbed. Small animals scurry to their burrows. None want to face the Everglades' apex predator.

But I do.

I angle my head to bare my neck to my fated mate. Despite my desire to be claimed, my body tenses as his mouth lowers. Instead of sharp fangs, soft lips press to the spot. Then he sits back. His hooded eyes regard me.

"Aren't you going to bite me?" I ask when my breath evens out.

Tag trails a fingertip along my neck and shoulder. The sensuous touch combined with his warm breath on my sweat-dampened skin makes me shiver. I mewl.

"Not tonight, my fated mate. We must prepare."

"THERE THEY ARE!"

I grin at my fated mate as she bounces beside me, pointing at the approaching helicopters. I chuckle to myself, as much from her excitement as my own.

During her call with the turned she-wolves, I sensed her emotions change from nervousness to happiness, then to strong desire. My own emotions mirrored hers. I decided a relaxing glass of Macallan Scotch would settle my nerves.

Giving her complete privacy, I stayed on the back deck. As she neared me, the level of awareness increased. The mate bond pulsed with her need for me. I sent mine of hers back. When she arrived at the sliding door and paused, I all but leaped to my feet and carried her caveman-style to our bedroom suite. But I maintained my control.

Her poignant words touched my very soul. I'll forever remember them and the expression of pure love on her beautiful face. Even now, my heart soars higher than the approaching helicopters. I squeeze her hand and grin wider than the Cheshire Cat.

"Yup, right on time! My boys always come through, babe."

After we made love on the deck and showered, we FaceTimed Jagger to give him the fantastic news. He and Sage congratulated us—him with a piercing wolf whistle and her with delighted squeals. Wren giggled while I beamed with masculine pride.

I patched Rust, Dylan, and Viggo in on the call.

Rust agrees it's best he oversees her transition. His medical experience will help her through it, if necessary. And like Jagger, he believes she will survive the process since we're fated mates. That's the one thing I didn't mention to her. No need to cause unnecessary panic. Plus, Sage confirms Wren will be a remarkable she-wolf, alleviating any residual concern. Natalie—Rust's fated mate—offered to help too, since she's a doctor.

Dylan and Viggo offer their support. We teased Viggo he's the last male standing. He scoffed and bragged he'll forever be a playboy. Sasha—Dylan's fated mate—congratulated us with a Russian saying for a happy, prosperous life.

For now, they're the only ones besides the pack members here we share the news with. Once Wren recovers from the transition, we'll announce our status to my parents and to the rest of the pack. They'll come to camp to witness our mate bonding ceremony. Afterwards, we'll celebrate with dinner and a pack run through the Everglades. Then I'll take my fated mate into seclusion for the rest of the month.

The helicopters land one after the other on the spacious helipad. The rotors slow as the doors open. My boys, their mates, and in Jagger and Dylan's cases, their pups emerge. I smile when Signy follows Sage, who carries Tove. Jagger's younger sister waves. I return the gesture with a grin. Judging by the shopping bags she carries, the pack princess fashionista wants to help Wren with her dress for the ceremony.

"Who's she? She looks familiar."

My fated mate's question draws me from my musings. I smile and tell her it's Signy, explaining how she used to accompany me to social events. Wren recalls her photos from the society columns. Yup, that's Signy.

I guide Wren forward. She raises her hand in greeting.

"Hey! Good to see you guys!" I say as I one-arm hug the guys and nod at the females, then step back. "Everybody, this is Wren Byrd, my fated mate."

Jagger inclines his head while Sage embraces her. The others approach and introduce themselves. The she-wolves with hugs, and the males with respectful nods. Even though we're best friends, males know better than to touch another's female. Wren's face glows with each greeting, and she coos at the pups.

We pile into the SUVs and drive back to camp. After they drop off their things, everyone comes to our cabin. They join Wren and me on the deck. Viggo heads to the outdoor kitchen to start up the grill for lunch. The others sit around the large oval table.

I pull a bottle of NV Billecart-Salmon Brut Rose Champagne—Wren's favorite—from the ice bath in the center. She claps as I pop the cork and fill her flute. Jagger opens another bottle. Once everyone has a glass, I take Wren's hand. She stands beside me, and we raise our glasses.

"My best friends, I thank you for joining my fated mate and me as I claim her, and she transitions. Your support and love are invaluable. We thank you."

"Hear, hear!"

"Congratulations!"

"*Vot vam!*"

"You sucker!"

Everyone cracks up at Viggo's declaration. I shake my head at the male two years younger than me.

"Give it time, bro. You'll be panting after some female soon."

"Yeah. And I hope she gives your sorry ass a hard time!" Dylan quips.

"Not me, bros!" Viggo responds as he tosses back his Champagne. He sets the flute on the table with a wink at Wren. "I hope you keep a happy smile on Mr. Grumpy's oh so cheery face, little sis!"

I throw a handful of ice at him.

He ducks, chuckling and heads to the grill.

"Meanwhile, I'll rustle up some grub, even for the latest sucker," he tosses over his shoulder.

Jagger glances at Rust. He turns to Dylan. I nod. Then the three of us bum rush Viggo. We knock him to the deck wrestling like we did as pups. He yelps and flails his arms. But we overpower him.

I leave the others holding him down and remove the bottles from the ice bath. I carry the oversized sterling silver bucket over to them. The guys step back, leaving Viggo on the deck. He raises his arms as I dump the water and ice on him. He shouts. We laugh.

"Get used to cold baths, bro. The she-wolf you'll lust after will give you blue balls!" Jagger guffaws.

The girls chastise us for being mean and offer Viggo help. They gather around him and help him to his feet. Over their heads, he winks at us. We growl.

"Thank you, my little sisters. Your mates and brother are savages. I shall return to the male's cabin, change, and return to cook you a delicious feast."

He bows his head. Water drips from the long copper strands. The girls fuss over him until he disappears around the side of the cabin.

"Not nice, Tag!" My fated mate chides, wagging her finger.

I grin and nip it.

She gasps as her pupils dilate.

"Stop right there," Jagger says. "We have details to discuss."

Reluctantly, I loosen my bite on her finger. I drape my arm over her shoulders and return to the table. The others join us. We leave the sun to melt the ice and to dry the water.

"This afternoon, I'll issue the claiming bite. That way, we have the rest of the day and evening to watch over Wren. Rust, you and Natalie will be on hand while I stay in the bedroom. I think it's best she recovers there than in the infirmary. What do you think?"

Rust and Natalie consider my plan. They glance at one another as though communicating silently. Then Rust answers.

"That's fine. Once you're showered and Wren wears something comfortable, call me. Nat and I will come over to check her vitals. We'll get a reading now, so we have a baseline. We'll stay in a guest suite. That way, we're close, even though only Jagger and Sage's cabin separate ours from yours. Time could be of the utmost importance."

I nod, then turn to Jagger.

"Alpha, what do you think?" I ask deferentially.

"It's a solid plan. Sage and I will stay in another guest suite for the same reason. In addition to Rust and Natalie's medical expertise, Sage will use her magick if necessary."

Wren's head whips towards me. Her eyebrows rise to her hairline. Mouth round.

"Magic?" She croaks. "Like a magician?"

I'd laugh at the comical sight. But I know she's surprised. I clasp her hand and turn to Sage.

"Not m-a-g-i-c, Wren. M-a-g-i-c-k as in witches."

Sage pauses to give Wren a moment to absorb her words. Wren blinks. Her eyes flick from Sage to mine and back. Sage smiles.

"Your drawings are not so far off, Wren. Wolves, others, and witches. You see, we're older than any of the other paranormal beings…"

Sage goes on to give Wren a brief history and ends with her formal titles. She also explains how she handled the fight situation and healed that fucker. My fated mate listens enraptured. Then she nods.

"Yesterday, the turned she-wolves told me you have an even more extraordinary experience of becoming a she-wolf. I wondered what they meant and planned to ask you about it. Would you mind?"

"Of course!"

While we listen to her story, Viggo returns. I feel a tad bit bad and help him to gather the platters of food from the kitchen. We have a major spread of salads, spicy sausages, lobster, shrimp kebabs, and steaks. I chuckle, recalling my fated mate's reaction to the alligators. Lunch is a carnivore's delight.

I leave our pack's master chef to do his thing and rejoin the others.

"Talk about a paranormal Romeo and Juliet!"

Wren exclaims as Sage nods. Jagger kisses her temple as

he wraps his arm around her. She nestles against him with a contented smile on her stunning face.

I take my fated mate's hand and kiss her cheek. That's the love I want for us—unbreakable. She smiles up at me, and my heart fills with the love she sends through our mate bond. I return mine to her. She cups my cheek.

"Enough with the lovebirds snugglefest. We have just as important plans to make. And time is of the essence!"

All eyes turn to Signy.

"Wren, the girls and I need to know what theme you want for your mate bonding ceremony and the dinner. We won't discuss your gown with you-know-who around. But the other stuff is fair game."

Sadness comes through the mate bond. I lift Wren's face. Tears fill her eyes.

"What's wrong, babe?"

She sucks in a sob and shakes her head.

"I just wish my parents were alive. My Dad would walk me down the aisle, and my Mom would help me pick out my dress. Even Maya can't be here," she finishes with a hiccup.

I dab her eyes with a linen napkin. The soothing rumble rises in my chest as my other hand rubs her back.

"Wren, I am so sorry about your parents. Unfortunately, we cannot allow humans to know of our existence except in cases such as yours. So, I can't do anything about your best friend. However, it would be my honor as your Alpha and friend to walk you down the aisle," Jagger says.

She covers her mouth with her hand and nods vigorously. Her emotions roll through our tether. I smile at Jagger in thanks. He nods.

"The rest of us share our condolences too, Wren. As for your friend, she may not be here. But there's no reason you can't retain your relationship with her after you transition. You can never reveal yourself or us to her," Sage says, then continues. "And as your Luna and friend, the girls and I will ooh and aah with you as you choose your gown. We'll help you prep too. Just as others did for me, Sasha, and Natalie."

The girls chime in their agreement.

"And…"

We turn to Dylan. He gestures at Jagger, Rust, and Viggo.

"The guys and I are your new big brothers. We vow to protect you with our lives. Should you ever need a thing, call and we will be there for you."

Wren's shoulders shake as tears spill down her flushed cheeks. She clears her throat and glances around the table.

"Thank you. Thank you all so much," she whispers.

Signy lightens the mood by steering the conversation to the ceremony and dinner. I zone out but continue to stoke my fated mate's back while I rumble low. She relaxes and talks excitedly about the plans.

I sense a stare and look up to find Jagger watching me. He nods his head, a satisfied expression on his face. I nod back.

After a while, Viggo calls for the girls to collect their lunch. The tantalizing aroma of the grilled meats makes my wolf sit up, tongue lolling. I agree. We're about to feast. Once they fill their plates, the guys get their portions. We thank Viggo for another delicious meal. He grins and raises his flute.

"May your bellies always be as full of good food as your hearts are with love."

The girls swoon.

Jagger glances at Rust. He turns to Dylan. I nod.

"LOSER!" We shout.

He winks as the girls smile adoringly at him.

Always a player.

~

Wren

"They're all so gorgeous! I don't know which one to pick!"

I widen my arms at the array of gowns Signy hung on racks in the sitting room of my bedroom suite.

She has superb taste. Not one would I cross off. They vary with hemlines from floor length with trains to ankle, midi, and above the knee. The fabrics range from silk to lace to chiffon. And she didn't stop there with options. The colors include the expected white and off-white. But the blush pink and floral gowns prove good competition for the traditional ones. All flatter my figure.

Signy bustles over. Her fingers flip through the gowns. She pauses at one, shakes her head, then continues her perusal. Then she snaps her fingers.

"This one! The floral chiffon gown is light and airy. Perfect for an outdoor ceremony in the humid Everglades evening. The plunging v neckline shows off your boobs while the waist cinches to accentuate your hour-glass figure. The draping detail lets the gown flow around you. You'll resemble an enchanted forest goddess!"

Signy's elaborate description hypes me up.

"Yes! I love it, thank you!"

The girls agree with claps and snaps of their fingers. We giggle and toast with Champagne.

"Now that you've chosen your gown, how do you envision the ceremony bower and table settings? It'll take place in the square before sunset," Sage asks.

"I'd love to incorporate the beauty of the Everglades."

She nods and an image shimmers before us. It solidifies to reveal the square decorated with columns of intertwined tree branches and wildflowers strung with thousands of fairy lights. They surround the area to allow for the celebration to continue after the sun sets. Amidst the garden and benches stand rows of long rectangular tables with pale green tablecloths and matching wooden chairs. Floral arrangements line the center with buckets of my favorite Champagne. Chafing dishes with a variety of foods and beverages sit on tables to the side. A separate table holds a four-tiered cake. A ceremony bower with the same treatment of wildflowers, tree branches, and fairy lights stands at one end.

"Oh, Sage, how beautiful," I breathe.

She smiles and says, "I kept it in the theme Natalie and I used for our ceremonies, but changed the colors. Let nature stand out. Plus, it goes along with your enchanted forest goddess gown. I'll have it all set up for you. Magick!"

She wiggles her fingers. We laugh.

"Okay, a male has but so much patience, you know!"

Our laughter bubbles over as Tag bellows outside the closed double doors. My teddy bear is morphing into Mr. Grumpy.

"Hold on a minute, Tag!" Sage calls out, then she does her thing, and the dresses disappear. She winks at me. "Well, Wren, enjoy your claiming!"

Sasha and Natalie titter. Signy rolls her eyes. They file out, making comments to Tag that make his cheeks redden. He glances at me over their heads. A thrill rushes through me.

This is it.

Tag closes the double doors and stalks towards me. His ravenous eyes lock on mine. Single-minded determination settles on his handsome face. The apex predator targets its prey. He moves with grace, persistent in his pursuit.

My heart pounds. My entire body quivers in need for this powerful male. I mewl as a blast of desire zips through our mate bond. It travels from my heart to my core. My lower belly heats from the intensity.

"Are you ready for me to make you mine in all ways, Wren Byrd?"

His deepened voice filled with passionate dominance skitters across my heated skin.

I moan a yes, holding my arms out to accept him—all of him.

He scoops me up with a growl and carries me into the bedroom. I slide down his body as he places me on my feet beside the bed. He grips the hem of my tunic and pulls it over my head. It drops to the floor as he unfastens my shorts. They slip down my thighs. I step out of them and kick them to the side. Naked, I stand before him.

His eyes darken with unchecked lust before they disappear behind his t-shirt, and he yanks it off. I rip the placket of his jeans. The buttons pop free. The head of his erect cock peeks out. I shove the jeans down his hips. He kicks them off.

He walks me backwards until I fall onto the bed. He flips me over and pulls my hips up until I rest on all fours. His palm slides up my spine, pushing between my shoulder blades. I lower to my forearms and toss my hair over a shoulder. He growls at my bared neck. I wiggle my ass. He spanks it with another growl. I groan as the erotic pain radiates through me. The moan deepens in my throat when he slams his cock inside my wet pussy.

Immediately, he sets a brutal pace. His groin slaps against my ass while his heavy balls kiss my engorged clit.

The pounding continues as our cries and musky scents fill the air. His cock expands. He increases to a frenzied pace. His arm bands around my waist. A hand grips my shoulder. He lowers his torso to my back, still thrusting. I cry out in surprise when the base of his cock expands and locks behind my pelvis. His knot! Just like my novels. I scream.

His warm breath huffs against my neck and shoulder. Warm liquid drips on the spot. I stiffen, knowing what comes next. A searing pain blanks my mind as his sharp fangs puncture my tender flesh.

"MINE!"

He growls like the wild beast he is. His mouth opens again, then clamps back down on the same spot. He shakes his head to deepen the claiming bite.

My skin sizzles. The serum rushes through my system just as his cock spurts his seed deep into my womb. My pussy contracts, milking his cock of every drop. I keen. Then all goes black.

"—BEEN four days. She doesn't eat. What's happening to her? I can't lose Wren!"

As Tag's anguished cries draw me from a dreamless slumber, I awake to pain in my chest and blinding light.

"T—Too bright..."

My words come out in a harsh voice. My dry throat makes it difficult to speak.

"Wren???"

"Tag."

The now darkened room explodes in cheers.

I'm pulled from soft pillows and crushed against his muscular chest. Hot tears spill in my hair. He cries my name over and over. The pain in my chest morphs to solace and happiness. I wrap my arms around my fated mate.

My fated mate!

"Did you say four days passed? Since you claimed me?"

"Yes," he replies gruffly.

"Tag, let me check Wren's vitals."

At a male's voice, I glance over Tag's shoulder to find Rust, Natalie, Jagger, and Sage standing around the bedroom. Tag growls. Rust holds up his hands, palms out. Natalie steps forward.

"Tag, I'll check her. Will you allow me?"

He nods and moves to sit beside me, one protective arm around my shoulders. His gaze flicks between the others and Natalie. Slowly, she approaches. I pat his thigh.

"My love, it's all right. I'm fine. In fact, I feel fantastic! It's okay for Natalie to check me. All right?"

He grunts his assent. The caveman.

I smile at Natalie and sit up. I notice a silk nightgown covers me. My beaded nipples press against the soft fabric. No wonder Tag freaked out at Rust! I pull the sheet up. Tag squeezes my shoulder.

Natalie checks my vitals, reflexes, eyes, and my hearing. When she's done, she declares I'm in perfect condition.

And I feel it. All senses heightened. The world is in sharp focus with amplified sound.

"Excellent news! Wren, you pulled through like a champ!" Jagger says as he smiles broadly.

"That's our girl!" Sage chimes in. "Now, for your mate bonding ceremony tomorrow. Whoohoo!"

I glance up at Tag and grin. He relaxes and grins back. He drops a kiss on the crown of my head, and I snuggle against his side.

"Well, that's our cue!" Rust says with a chuckle. He takes Natalie's hand and heads for the door.

"We'll have food sent over for you. They'll knock and leave it at the door," Sage says as Jagger places his hand on the small of her back.

He nods and ushers her from the bedroom.

Before the sitting room doors close, Tag pounces. I giggle and wrap my arms around him.

"You're truly okay, baby?"

"Absolutely! I've never felt better. And I see my she-wolf on the periphery. Will you show me how to shift?"

He nuzzles my neck, kissing the claiming bite that's already healed.

"Yes, and so much more."

I shiver at the inference in his words, especially since he nudges my thighs apart with his knees. I widen my legs to cradle him against me. We spend the next few hours doing *so much more.*

～

"We're so happy for you and our son, Wren!"

"Yes, darling, welcome to our family and to our pack!"

I promised I wouldn't cry on my mate bonding ceremony day. But the kind words from Branson and Ylva—Tag's parents—choke me up. Tears shine in my eyes as I return their embraces. Tag rubs my back when I return to his side and hold his hand.

First a fated mate and new friends, then a new family and a whole pack. I'm the luckiest girl in the world.

"Thank you so much! I feel so lucky to have all of you in my life, especially my fated mate," I respond as I look up at him.

I raise to my tippy toes to kiss his lips when I notice tears shimmering in my teddy bear's eyes. He wraps his arms around me and lifts me as he deepens the kiss. When he finally puts me down, I peek at his parents.

They beam at us. I smile back, so elated.

"We hate to interrupt your first introduction. But we have to get Wren ready for their ceremony."

Sage enters the great room with Signy, Sasha, and Natalie. They grin and beckon me with crooked fingers.

I laugh and kiss Tag on the cheek, then extend my hand to Ylva.

"I would love for you to join us."

She smiles and clasps my hand.

Jagger, Dylan, Rust, and Viggo enter and take Tag away for some kind of bro bonding. Branson declines their invitation and heads to the clubhouse to meet up with the older males.

After a couple of hours being pampered by pack aestheticians, the girls help me to dress. Sage uses a glamour spell for my hair and makeup. I twirl in the trifold mirror, grinning at my reflection. Jagger comes, and it's time to meet Tag at the ceremony bower. Jagger helps me into a golf cart while the others follow in separate carts.

"So, you're truly happy with everything, Wren?"

"Yes, Alpha, so thrilled. Thank you for welcoming me to your pack."

"*Our* pack. And you're more than welcome. You make an excellent addition."

I smile all the way down the aisle where my handsome fated mate waits for me to exchange our vows.

"Wren Byrd, I claim you as my fated mate to protect, love, and cherish for all time. To bear my pups and to stand by my side. I love you, Wren Dahl, my fated mate!"

He slips a ginormous emerald-cut diamond ring set in platinum on my finger. It glints in the sun. He assures me when we shift back, jewelry reappears intact.

I swallow back tears of joy, then clear my throat to respond.

"Tag Dahl, I claim you as my fated mate to protect, love, and cherish for all time. To bear your pups and to stand by my side. I love you, Tag Dahl, my fated mate!"

I slip a platinum band on his ring finger.

The clearing explodes with shouts and howls of jubilation.

Tag scoops me in his arms. I throw my head back and let my she-wolf howl with her joy. Tag joins us for a song of love. Then he carries me back up the aisle to the pack's shouts and howls of celebration reaching the sky. He sets me down next to our table and kisses me senseless. The voices of others as they take their seats don't stop my male from claiming my mouth.

"When the happy couple comes up for air, we can toast their new bond."

I laugh against Tag's lips. He nips my lower one and stands to his full height.

"We're ready, Alpha."

Jagger chuckles. He and Sage raise their Champagne flutes. We follow their lead.

"Miami Wolves Pack, tonight we welcome our newest member, Wren Dahl, to our family—"

Everyone cheers. Once they settle down, he continues.

"She is Tag's fated mate. Once human, she fully transitioned to a she-wolf."

The pack murmurs their congratulations.

"Tonight, we celebrate Tag and Wren's mate bonding with good food and fellowship, followed by a pack run. Join Sage and me in welcoming Wren to our pack!"

I push back the tears and laugh as the square fills with the pack's howls. Tag cups my cheek and kisses me until my toes curl. More howls and whistles fill the air.

"Now, we eat, drink, and be merry!"

Jagger exclaims and downs his Champagne, then he and Sage sit.

While we eat, each pack member introduces themselves and congratulates us on our bonding and me on my successful transition. The three turned she-wolves intro-duce me to their fated mates. I hug the females and tell them their kind words helped tip the scales in favor of me accepting Tag and being a wolf-shifter. He thanks them and claps their mates on the back.

As we dance, Tag tells me how gorgeous I am. My heart swells with gladness. After we eat the cake, the sun sets. Jagger announces the time for the pack run. I glance at Tag nervously. He brushes his lips against mine and murmurs how he believes in me.

While the pack strips and shifts amidst crackles and flashes, I slip out of my gown and sandals. No one pays attention to my nakedness or comments on my size, espe-cially amongst the sleek and lithe she-wolves. Tag clasps my chin between his thumb and index finger.

"You are my beautiful fated mate. No one compares to you, Wren Dahl. Now shift for me, baby."

At his command, my body morphs into my mahogany brown she-wolf. I embrace the now familiar shift and the wolf. I tilt my head up to stare at my fated mate, then tip it further to howl with the others. Pride from Tag fills my heart through our mate bond. I lower my head and find his giant sable haired wolf before me.

He throws his head back and howls, then nudges my flank with his snout. He races past me to join our Alpha and Luna at the head of the pack. I follow to take my place by his side as the mate of the beta. My new family parts to let me through.

As I approach with head bowed, our Alpha and Luna

bark in acceptance while the beta stands tall. Then our Alpha turns, followed by our Luna. My mate yips at me and follows.

I race after them, overjoyed to have a genuine family again.

ag

"I THINK I'll leave my social clothes at the duplex. Wherever we go will be based on the mainland, anyway. I can get dressed there. Oh, and I'll leave makeup and stuff. I'm so glad we're keeping that residence so I can hang out with Maya there. It won't be like I'm lying. It's still our home and my office."

I try hard to pay attention to my fated mate. But she's bent over in her walk-in closet in our Moon Island bedroom suite. The bottom curves of her generous ass play hideand-seek in the skimpy shorts. My mouth waters.

"Tag? Are you even listening to me?"

She spins around and straightens with her hands on her hips. Her face set in a scowl until she sees mine full of lust.

"Oh, no, mister! You've kept me tied to the bed for twelve whole days and nights. You're insatiable. Not that I mind. But now, I want to get settled in my new home. Promise me you'll behave."

I'm tempted to say after one more round. But she arches an eyebrow and folds her arms under her succulent tits. Now, my mouth salivates for their plump juiciness. But I shake my head to clear the carnal thoughts.

"Fine. However, if I help you, you'll finish faster. Then we—"

"Ah, ah. Nope. You'll just distract me with all that sexiness you have going on. Give me ninety minutes, then you can ravish me," she says with a wink. "Now, go. Hang out with Dylan. He and Sasha just returned from their time in New York City. She says he's caught up in an MMA video game. Since he fights for real, he acts like he's the players. You can work off some tension playing the game."

Not a bad suggestion. I pull out my mobile, tap on the screen, and turn it to face her.

She frowns and steps closer. Her tinkling laughter fills the closet.

"Tag Dahl! You are such a stickler. A ninety-minute countdown? Give me a break."

I smirk and wave the mobile in the air as I back out of the closet ticking down the seconds. She waves her hands to shoo me out as she giggles. I shout the latest number when I reach the double doors of the sitting room. She shouts for me to get a life.

I chuckle. She is my life. And I've already got her.

At the bottom of the steps, my mobile rings. It's Rust.

"Hey—"

"Listen, come to the ER. Wren's uncle just came in. Heart attack. I'm the attending. Gotta go."

The call ends. I race up the stairs four at a time, calling her name. She runs into the hallway.

"What—"

"Your uncle had a heart attack. We gotta go, now!"

Her eyes widen.

I grab her hand and pull her back to her closet. I help her switch out of the booty shorts into jeans and flats. She takes off the t-shirt and puts on a bra, then replaces it. I glance around for her mobile and notice three missed calls. She has it on silent. Damn! I grab her wallet and a bag, shoving everything inside. I take her hand and hurry for the garage.

While we zip towards the hospital, she checks her voice messages. They're all from her aunt. Tears stream down my fated mate's cheeks as she talks to her. He's in surgery. They were at the club playing golf. He collapsed. She tells her aunt we'll be there soon and ends the call.

I rub her thigh as I rumble in my chest. She remains silent, staring out the window. We pull into the parking lot near the emergency room entrance. I slide the Bentayga into a spot. Wren jumps out before I can get to her. She runs towards the sliding doors. I catch up to her easily and race through the doors beside her. A nurse directs us to the waiting room. We hurry down the crowded hallway, dodging gurneys and staff. We burst through the door. Wren spots her aunt and rushes over.

"Any word?" She asks, sitting next to the older woman.

She glances up with red-rimmed eyes. Her face puffy and tearstained. She shakes her head and covers her mouth as she sobs into a wet handkerchief.

Wren wraps her arms around her as tears stream down her face. Despite the woman's mean behavior towards her, my fated mate still shows compassion. I send soothing vibes through our mate bond. She glances up at me with a watery smile.

"I'll go see what I can find out. Rust is the attending physician. Maybe Natalie can get us some answers."

Wren nods and continues to console her aunt.

I jog to the nurses' station. They can't give me information since I'm not listed as kin. I stifle a growl and whip out my mobile. Natalie answers on the first ring.

"Hi—"

"We're in the ER. Wren's uncle had a heart attack. Rust is the attending. I can't get the nurses to tell me anything. Can you find out?"

"I'm on my way."

"Thanks."

As I return to the waiting room, the mate bond pulses with anger. What the hell?! I race to the room.

That fucker is arguing with my fated mate. Here we go again. But this time, I control myself and my wolf—even though he snarls viscously.

"—off, Jonathan. Now is not the time for your nonsense! Leave me alone."

Wren whisper yells at the fool. But I can hear her clearly across the room.

"If your uncle dies—"

She slaps him so hard, his head snaps sideways. I may be in control of my wolf. But hers flashes in her eyes. I rush to her side and block her with my body from him. Then I reach back to put a hand on her arm. I glare down at the fucker, who's seven inches shorter.

"Get the hell out of here, or I will have security escort you off the premises."

He glares up at me.

"Who the hell are you?"

My lip curls as I snarl, "Wren's pissed husband. Now. Get. The. Fuck. Out."

He balks. Then moves to the side to glance at her around me. I move with him, keeping her safely behind my body.

"Is there a problem here?"

I maintain eye contact with him and use my periphery to see the newcomer. It's a security guard with Natalie. I nod.

"Yes. This jerk is not a member of the family and needs to be escorted from the premises."

The guard takes him by the arm and leads him away as he shouts obscenities.

I turn to my fated mate.

"Are you okay?"

She nods. I'm thankful her eyes returned to their mink brown.

"I'll go check the chart and come back," Natalie says and hurries away.

I guide Wren back to her aunt, who shakes her head.

"So uncouth."

Yeah.

Natalie returns and tells us all the information she can find out, which isn't much since he's still in the operating room. But she stays with us since it's the end of her day. We wait in silence.

Hours later, Rust comes out. He strides towards us. I gauge his body language and note the tension around his eyes and in the set of his shoulders. I take Wren's hand in mine.

"Mrs. Byrd, Wren, he's stable. But it'll be a while before you can see him. He's being transported to the ICU. I wanted to come to you as soon as I could. His heart suffered extensive damage and with his age, we can't give a definitive prognosis at this time. However, we did our best. Now, we wait for his body to heal. Do you have any questions?"

Her aunt asks if she can see him through the window. Rust says he'll check with the ICU. Then his pager goes off. Her aunt gasps. But he shakes his head and tells her it's another patient. He leaves, promising to have word from the ICU sent to them and a nod at Natalie.

"I'll check for you," she offers and leaves the waiting room.

"You know, Wren, your uncle loves you dearly. You may not think so. But he does. So do I. We just want what's best for you," she glances at me and nods. "I know who you are. You make a good match for Wren. I was never fond of Jonathan."

My fated mate's eyes widen in shock.

Her aunt pats her arm and falls silent again.

WREN

"YOU CAN GO in to see him now, Wren."

I nod at Aunt Gretchen.

She's aged these past eight days. The stress of waiting for Uncle George to awake from the induced coma added wrinkles around the corners of her eyes and between her eyebrows normally Botoxed smooth. Still fashionable, she wears Chanel from head to toe—a sheath dress with a cardigan around her shoulders and ballet flats. She reaches into her 2.55 handbag and pulls out a handkerchief to dab her eyes.

My heart clenches. I glance up at Tag. He offers an encouraging smile. I rise from the sofa in the hospital ante-room of Uncle George's private suite and head towards the bedroom. At the door, I glance over my shoulder at my fated mate. He smiles and nods his head. I enter the room.

The beeping machines and antiseptic products assail my new enhanced senses. I shake my head as my nose wrinkles. The raspy sound of my name brings my attention to the bed.

Uncle George lies on his back with the bed adjusted so it's elevated. Tubes stick in his nose and hands. He appears frail and swallowed up by the bedding. But his eyes still hold their light, even if dim.

I walk over and sit on the chair beside the bed.

"Hello, Uncle George. Don't speak. I won't stay long. I just want to let you know I'm here and hope you get better."

He lifts his finger resting beside him. My eyes drop to a legal-size manila envelope next to it. My name—written in bold lettering—stands out. Surprised, I lift my gaze back to his face.

He opens his mouth. But words don't come out.

"No. No. I'll get it," I say as I reach for the envelope.

I open it and scan the contents. It's a copy of his will. And I'm still the sole heir. I inherit all, including Byrd Capital. A separate fund provides Aunt Gretchen with a monthly allotment until her death, then the fund reverts to me. I stare in shock.

"Uncle George, thank you. But we'll table this for a much later time. You focus on improving your health. I'll visit you every day. Now, get some rest."

He stares at me for a long moment. Then his eyes flutter closed. His breathing remains steady.

As horrible as he treated me, I do not wish him any harm. I return to my fated mate, take his hand, and bid Aunt Gretchen a good night. I tell her I'll see her in the morning. Then leave with the male whose love I never have to question.

CHAPTER 19

ren

"NO! Absolutely not, Wren Dahl! Skip yourself right back up those stairs and put on some real clothes. I kid you not, female."

My fated mate thunders as I stand on the bottom step in our duplex. I spent the day with Maya. So, Tag met me here.

We're about to leave for Club Hati—one of Larson Enterprises' exclusive dance clubs—for our first Date Night with Sage, Jagger, Sasha, Dylan, Natalie, and Rust. We invited Viggo. But he declined, not wanting to be *the ninth wheel*.

I feel bad for him since he's the only one not mated out

of his brother and best friends. When I asked him about it, he winked at me and said he doesn't mind multiples, just not with males. I chucked him on the shoulder. He grinned with sparkling ice blue eyes. The handsome billionaire playboy would rather continue to play than to mate. He's the youngest of the guys. So, who could blame him?

I'm young too and want to look sexy despite my fated mate's protest. I glance down at my merlot colored mini dress.

It's short and flirty. The pleated bodice with a halter neckline and revealing open back gives way to a softly pleated skirt that skims my thighs. A wide, laser-cut belt nips in my waist. The black leather contrasts nicely with the mini dress' rich color and softness. Paired with sky-high strappy stilettos, the mini dress and shoes lengthen my newly toned legs. All that running around as a she-wolf and wrapping my legs around my bucking bronco trimmed them better than squats!

I glance back up at Tag and pout my glossy pink lips. Sashaying forward, I bat my eyelashes at him, purring in my chest.

"Oh, my love, I wore this for you," I say, then spin in a slow circle making the skirt lift to reveal my bare booty. Facing him, I continue. "So, while we're grinding on the dance floor, your hands can roam freely. No encumbrances."

I step into him. My breasts press against his eight-pack abs. I tilt my head back to pin him with a sultry gaze. His cock twitches against my lower belly. With my fingertips, I trace his sculpted chest beneath the black v-neck silk sweater. They swirl around his nipples and tweak them. His chest vibrates with a growl. My sensuous exploration continues as I trail my fingertips up to press against his mouth.

"Do I not please you, Sir?"

The growl increases as he nips my fingers. I yelp and draw them back. But he grasps my wrists and sucks on the digits. Smoldering eyes bore into me. He pulls my fingers from his mouth with a pop. While his eyes remain on mine, his tongue darts out to lick the length of each finger. Then he closes his hand around them and strides to the double doors.

"We leave now, you Siren. Or, I will have my way with you on *this* floor, not the one in the club."

My body thrums. But I want to go out with our friends more than to party in the sheets at home. We'll have plenty of time to get our groove on. So, I all but skip behind him with a satisfied grin on my face.

Tag helps me into the Wraith. As he shuts the door, my mobile rings. I slip it out of my sequined clutch and check the screen. It's Sage.

"Hey, we're in the car now. Where are you guys?"

"Oh, good. We just turned onto the causeway. Instead of taking separate cars, we're in the Sprinter. See you in a few!"

She ends the call as Tag slips behind the steering wheel.

"That was Sage. They're on their way now, too. I can't wait to dance. Whoop, whoop!"

My fated mate chuckles as he drives towards the garage's exit. We arrive in no time.

The sedan stops in front of an Art Deco building in a prime spot located on Ocean Drive that offers unobstructed views of the Atlantic Ocean. The building stands three stories with a rooftop lounge and has a sleek linear appearance with stylized ornamentation. A sectioned-off outdoor area offers seating for dining and drinking at the bar.

Two men in custom-tailored black suits flank the entry. A queue extends around the corner of people in expensive attire patiently awaiting admittance to the club. Not surprising given Club Hati is for the über-wealthy and influential, too refined to behave boorishly. The hopeful patrons are not rambunctious as one would ordinarily see waiting outside a South Beach nightclub.

One doorman opens my door while a valet waits for Tag to emerge from his side.

"Welcome to Club Hati, Wren," the doorman says extending his arm.

They're members of our pack. The doormen are enforcers, perfect to handle any issues at the club should they arise.

I place my hand on his arm, and he lifts me from the seat. Did I say they're huge? Taller and bulkier than Tag. I thank the doorman as my fated mate removes my hand from his arm with a low growl. The doorman bows his head respectfully to the beta and wishes us a good evening.

I don't comment on Tag's possessive behavior. He's already none too pleased with my mini dress And I want to have fun tonight. He leads me through the outdoor area to the front doors. I notice women watch him appreciatively. My she-wolf and I snarl. Mine!

"Now, you know how I feel, Siren," he murmurs in my ear. "So, behave."

I huff as we enter the club. My she-wolf howls.

The air vibrates with the pulse of the music. The scent of expensive perfume and cologne mixes with an enticing aroma the club pumps through the ventilation system. Colorful lights change periodically.

My gaze roams around the lavish club full of the glitterati. Celebrities, socialites, fashionistas, and billionaire tycoons wear their sexiest, most revealing outfits. With my enhanced senses, I distinguish wolf shifters from humans easily. Bottles of top-shelf liquor and magnums of champagne sit atop the tables in the VIP booths. Assigned female servers in figure-fitting white tube mini dresses carry bottles with sparklers. The patrons applaud.

Those not fortunate to have a booth stand two deep at the three bars or perch on stools at high-top tables surrounding the dance floor. Bartenders stay busy serving drinks to those gathered.

The dance floor teems with gyrating bodies. Females dressed in more revealing outfits than mine dance with hot males. Partiers shake their things.

My clutch taps to the beat against my thigh as I follow Tag. He weaves through the crowd, a head above most others. I can't see beyond his back, but I know we reach our friends when I hear Jagger's greeting.

I step from behind Tag and wave. They cheer and raise their cocktail glasses in the air. A server offers Tag and me a tray of drinks. We select a scotch and a mojito, then raise our glasses in a toast with our friends.

"Here's to the first of many Date Nights with awesome friends!"

Everyone seconds Jagger's declaration before we sip our drinks.

Tag sits on a leather banquet and guides me to his lap. He tugs at the hem of my mini dress when it rides up my thighs. I lean over and whisper in his ear all the filthy things I want him to do to me. When I add on the dance floor, his cock thumps beneath my butt. I wiggle my hips and purr.

"Come on, girls, let's dance for our boys!"

Natalie rouses me from an almost-sex-induced thrall.

I wink at my fated mate and give my clutch to him. Sasha takes my hand and tugs. I rise and follow her with the others to the dance floor.

The DJ's music and callouts have everyone bouncing to the beat. I throw my hands up and shake my hips. In the crowd, no one will notice how high my mini dress rises. But I know Tag will. I twirl and bump my hip against Sage's. She giggles and shimmies.

"The DJ plays the best music!" She says as she bumps her hip against Natalie's side.

Sasha flips her waist-length ash blonde hair over her shoulder as she twirls on the dance floor. Her dove gray eyes—like her silver chain-mail micro mini dress—sparkle in the lights.

We move to the sensuous pulse of the music. A few males make their way over to us. We shake our heads and form a tight circle. Who's interested in any others when you have sexy as sin fated mates? The males take the hint and move on to more willing partners.

I lift my gaze towards the DJ, then shout.

Maya dances on a platform next to his booth. Lost in her own world, she has her eyes closed and moves seductively to the beat. She must have changed her mind from when I asked her to come with us earlier.

"That's Maya, my best friend. I'm going to get her," I tell Sage as I point. She nods, and I make my way through the throng of dancers.

Maya doesn't see me. But the DJ does. I gesture at her. He nods. A moment later, he strides over and taps her, then points at me. Her eyes widen, and she waves me up. I turn and point at the others. Maya nods and waves for them to come up, too.

A bouncer helps us navigate the steps in our high heels. I throw my arms around Maya's neck. We hug. Then I introduce her to the others. She grins and hugs them too. She goes to the DJ and whispers in his ear. He nods. She returns and winks at me.

Soon the music blends to T.I.'s "Live Your Life."

Giggling, I hug my bestie.

We turn to the others and start dancing as I belt out Rihanna's lyrics.

I have the best of both worlds. My fated mate and our pack and my best friend and work. What could be better?

EPILOGUE

wo Months Later
Tag

HERE WE GO AGAIN. When will they learn to not test my patience? I pin the presenter for the new hotel project with a disdainful look. He gulps.

"You do realize the hotel is a historic property in a historic district. Zoning does not allow any changes to the building's facade. Did you not get the memo?"

I cock an eyebrow and wait for whatever excuse he comes up with. And he doesn't disappoint.

He blathers on about wording in the zoning document he suggests we use to *get around the rule.* I let him keep talking to dig himself deeper into a pit from which he will never rise.

Those gathered around the table stare at him incredulously. Some appear to will him to shut up. Others lower their gazes. None want to incur the beast's wrath.

Sure, I'm not as harsh post-Wren. She pointed out how I could be a little less grumpy. I try my best to satisfy my fated mate. So, the whispers of me being a bosshole have lessened.

But my patience is already thin since Wren hasn't been well these past few days. It's unusual since she's a wolf shifter now. But since she's a transitioned and not a born she-wolf, we can't compare her healing abilities with theirs. Anomalies can happen.

If she doesn't feel better, she promises to ask Natalie to examine her when she finishes her day at the hospital. But, that's hours from now.

I glance at my watch for the hundredth time since this meeting started. Another thirty minutes to go. Then I have more meetings to attend. I can't believe of all the days, this one has back-to-back appointments. The last site visit is across town. So, it'll take a while to get back to Moon Island. Damn!

A polite cough brings my attention back to the conference room.

"I missed that last part. Repeat it."

The presenter blinks like a scared rabbit at my gruff command. He gathers himself and drones on.

With a sigh, I pay attention.

As soon as the meeting ends, I jump from my chair and stride out of the room, mobile to my ear. Wren answers on the first ring.

"Hi, my love."

The annoyance fades as her voice soothes me. I never expected to fall in love, and now I can't live without the love of my fated mate. A smile spreads across my face.

"Hi, to you, babe. How do you feel?"

She goes quiet.

I stop in the middle of the hallway. My heart thuds in my chest. Is the transition reversing? Is she experiencing side effects months later? Does she need another claiming bite?

"Talk to me, Wren. You've got me losing my mind here, babe."

"No, no! Nothing to worry about. I'm fine. I feel better, in fact," she responds, then continues. "But don't you have a ton of meetings to attend? Don't let me keep you. Get your work done, Mr. Dahl, Sir."

Relief weakens my knees. I brace a hand against the wall and hang my head. This female is going to kill me. My blood pressure lowers, and I continue to my office suite.

"You take priority over all, my fated mate. Never forget that. But I do need to go," I say as Beth looks at me expectantly with a file folder in her hands.

"I love you," Wren whispers. "See you when you get home."

A tug at our mate bond causes me to rub my chest. Beth averts her eyes. I take the folder and stride into my office, shutting the door.

"I love you, too," I reply gruffly and end the call.

I turn at the knock on my door. It opens, and Jagger pokes his head in.

"Ready to go?"

"Yeah, let me grab my laptop."

Hours later, I climb out of the Bentayga and tell my driver I won't need him or my security team tomorrow. It's Friday. I'll work from home and keep an eye on Wren.

Inside our mansion, I pause and listen for my fated mate. I don't want to call her name in case she's taking a nap. Besides not feeling well, she sleeps more.

No sound of her on the first floor. I bound up the stairs and stride towards our bedroom suite. The double doors stand closed. I open them softly and stick my head in. I glance around the sitting room. She's not on the sofa. Her scent is faint. But not strong enough to suggest she's in the bedroom.

I close the doors and spin on my heel. Then I notice the door to the closest guest bedroom suite stands open. I frown, wondering why she's in there. My ears detect a scratching sound. I hurry my steps.

The furniture in the room is gone except for a table with her sketchpad and a bottle of water. She wears one of my long-sleeve t-shirts and sits cross-legged on the floor in front of the largest wall. The pencil in her hand makes the scratching sound as she draws on the surface. She's so focused, she doesn't notice my approach.

Not wanting to startle her, I whisper her name. Her head snaps around anyway. Then she smiles and rises.

"Oh, you scared me! I didn't hear you," she says as she stretches her back and walks towards me.

"Sorry, babe," I murmur against her lips as she tilts her face up. After a soft kiss, I cup her cheek. "How do you feel? Did you go see Natalie at the island's hospital? What are you doing in here, anyway?"

She giggles and presses a finger to my lips.

"One question at a time. Although I must say, they're related," she replies, smiling broadly. "First, I want to show you something."

She leads me to the table and points at a drawing on the page. A male and a female wolf romp with three pups amongst pine trees near a marsh remarkably similar to the Everglades. It's so realistic, I could reach out and touch their fur or hear the playful growls of the exuberant pups. She points at the date. It's months ago. Before that unfortunate night of the gala.

"Remember, I mentioned how Sage flipped through my sketchpad after the gala?" She asks, then continues when I nod. "This is one of them she saw and found it curious I drew such a picture. I didn't know about you being a wolf shifter. But wolves dominated my dreams. I drew this and didn't think any more about it. Until today."

She glances up at me with tears in her eyes.

My heart lurches to my throat. I bite my lower lip to keep from speaking, wanting to hear her say it. But afraid I'm wrong.

She gestures towards the wall and the beginnings of a

mural replicating the drawing. Then she widens her arms to encompass the entire room.

"I thought this room with the wall taken down to open it to the one next door would make the perfect"—she takes my hand and places it under the t-shirt against her warm skin—"nursery for our three pups."

Her voice waivers as tears slip down her cheeks.

My mouth gapes as my eyes fill with tears. I can't speak. I drop to my knees and lift the t-shirt. As I stare at her rounded belly, the tears flow.

She twines her fingers in my hair. Her soothing purr reaches my ears. Our mate bond floods with love and joy.

I lift my gaze to her face.

"Y—You're pregnant... with my pups? T—Three of them?"

She nods, then gnaws the corner of her bottom lip. Her beautiful face glows. Eyes radiant with love.

I wrap my arms around her hips and press three kisses to her belly filled with my three pups. My eyes close as my forehead leans against her warm, soft skin.

She strokes my hair and asks, "Are you happy, my love?"

As I rise to my feet, I lift her in my arms and swing her around. I let out a jubilant howl. My fated mate giggles and throws her head back to join me. Our wolves take up the call. The cries echo around the empty nursery. Soon it will ring with the sweet coos of our precious pups. My heart soars higher than the moon above.

"Am I happy? Unbelievably ecstatic! You make me the luckiest male in the universe and beyond, Wren Dahl! I love you more than the air I breathe. You complete me, my fated mate. You and our pups mean more to me than you can ever imagine. Thank you, my love."

"I love you and our pups so much. Thank you, Tag Dahl, for not giving up on us. I've never been happier in my whole life."

She cups my face and covers my mouth with hers. I hold her aloft and return her kiss with unbridled passion.

And this is what I live for. My fated mate's happiness and now our pups.

They're my greatest wins.

THANK you for reading *Tag The Redemption: A Wolf Shifter Fated Mates Paranormal Romance*!

If you enjoyed the book, I would so appreciate your review as they make a huge difference for indie authors. Be sure to sign up for my newsletter for the latest info about the series, new releases, and a FREE book at **bit.ly/ CLBooksDylanTheRogue**! Next up: *Viggo The Obsession: A Wolf Shifter Fated Mates Paranormal Romance*. Turn the page for a preview of *Jagger The Temptation* and Viggo.

PREVIEW JAGGER THE TEMPTATION: A WOLF SHIFTER FATED MATES PARANORMAL ROMANCE

 agger

"THE QUARTERLY NUMBERS show an increase in profits. More than projected because of the opening of the beachfront resort in Charleston earlier than planned. The general manager reports the property sold out for the first four months..."

I nod as my Vice President of Hotels and Resorts for Larson Enterprises, Inc. continues his update. My mind focuses partially on his presentation.

For the last few weeks, I can't seem to focus. I don't know whether lack of sleep causes the lapse or something else. Dreams of another dominate my nights. They remain just out of reach, on the fringes. But it's their silent pleas for help that keep me tossing. A vibration from them of fear and sadness draws me closer. My instinct kicks in, and I want to save them, protect them.

Each dream brings me closer to them. But they remain just out of reach. I wake tangled in silk sheets. An arm extended as my hand reaches for them. Last night I called a name. However, as the last vestiges of the dream slipped away, the name dissolved with it.

I growl low in my chest in frustration.

My COO shifts his gaze to me. His wolf senses picked up my displeasure with ease.

I shake my head at Tag Dahl.

He cocks his head at me.

As my best friend, he's known me since we were pups. Born within a few weeks of each other—him to our pack's enforcer and me to our Alpha—Tag knows me as well as I know myself. I haven't mentioned my dreams to him, not that he'd think me nuts. No. I just don't know what they mean and if they warrant a conversation for analysis.

And Tag would delve into their meaning.

As my beta, he's my right-hand man. Anything that involves me and can impact our pack, he wants to solve the puzzle.

But this one will remain under wraps until I figure it out. So, I shake my head again and turn my attention back to the presentation. Even as I will my mind to pay full attention. I remove my personal hat. Then I firmly affix the one for my roles as CEO and Chairman of the Board of the luxury hotels, fine dining, clubs, and lounges company my family founded in Miami.

An hour later, a persistent Tag strides along with me to my suite of offices in The Larson Tower on Biscayne Bay. We pass through the executive floor as staff—wolf shifter and human—acknowledge us. The unaware humans often stare in awe at our formidable sizes. We're both six feet, seven inches of pure muscle and move with predatory grace. We nod in return but continue without pause.

I know Tag wants to find out what's up with me. I'll allow his henpecking since we're so close. Otherwise, I do not tolerate others in my business. No. One.

"Alpha, you have a few voicemails, sir."

"Thanks, Ginny," I respond to my administrative assistant as I open the double doors of my office. "Kindly hold my calls."

"What's up, Jagger?"

I bite back an irritated growl—lack of sleep will have you pissed, even at your best friend who only wants to help.

"You want a drink?" I ask as I unbutton the jacket of my bespoke three-piece Brioni suit and stride to the bar cart. It's after five-thirty, and I can use a stiff one before I head out to Club Sol & Mani for some much-needed sexual relief.

"Sure, thanks."

I take my time pouring two fingers of scotch into the Baccarat crystal tumblers. Absolutely no rush to have Tag pick at my psyche. My ears pick up his almost silent huff, and I chuckle to myself.

"Don't delay this conversation, Jag. You've been off for a few weeks now, and I've given you space," he says, then nods his thanks for the liquor. "What's up with you?"

Again, I allow him to question me, even though I'm his Alpha and my word is final.

I lower myself onto the dove gray tufted leather sofa in the seating area. Tag takes a chair opposite and places an ankle over a knee. I sip my drink as I consider my words. He knows better than to interrupt at this point.

"Dreams."

He cocks his head at the simple one-worded response. I shrug and take another sip.

"For the past few weeks, dreams invade my sleep. Every. Single. Night. Someone's in trouble. But I can't catch their name or where they are to help them," I sigh and stare out the window.

The panoramic view across Biscayne Bay with jet skiers and megayachts on its dazzling surface out to the azure Atlantic Ocean helps to quiet the inner turmoil my wolf and I sense. He turns his massive silvery white head to stare at me with accusatory ice blue eyes. It's as though he knows something I don't and pissed I'm not aware. I run my fingers through my white blond hair as I think on it, then shake my head. No clue.

"What do you recall?" Tag asks as he leans forward and places his elbows on his knees, the scotch tumbler balanced between his sizable hands.

I shrug.

"A brightness in the background prevents a clear view. I know it's outdoors since I hear the hum of insects and feel the warm sun on my skin. Naked skin. So, I must have shifted and returned to my human form."

Another sip of scotch, and I stand to pace my office.

Instinct tells me these are no ordinary dreams. But each morning I account for the whereabouts of my pack, and no one turns up missing. Not knowing who calls for my help drives me and my wolf mad.

I growl and toss back the rest of my scotch. A few long strides and I refill the tumbler.

"No one in our pack seems in trouble. I'll stop by the she-wolves' residences on my way home just to make sure. A few of our unmated males flew to New Orleans for the weekend. I'll shoot a text to them and make sure they didn't get into anything on Bourbon Street."

With a nod of agreement, I hold the decanter up. Tag declines a refill—ever the responsible one. Fine. It's not like wolf shifters can get drunk. Well, not too much. Our systems process substances differently from humans. All the better for us, especially when I'm in this pissy mood.

"Well, you know they say fated mates can have dreams about the other. The more frequent and intense they become, the closer the pair gets to their first encounter," Tag says. His emerald green eyes scan my face for a reaction. He knows I've waited all these years for my fated mate—and will continue to do so.

Despite my father's damn near daily persistence, I issue

the claiming bite and complete the mating bond with a single she-wolf. The last eleven years of nearly nonstop mating runs, with the she-wolves in my pack and those from nearby cities—hell, even overseas. Or galas at our hotels and mixers at our clubs, an accidental encounter, all to persuade me to select a she-wolf as my mate. None of them tempt me in the slightest.

All the she-wolves desire to bond with me. Then the supposed prince—and they were eager to lose their slippers and thongs for me to pick up——now the Alpha of the Miami Wolves Pack. Correction, *Billionaire Wolves of Miami* as the other packs refer to us. With good reason, since we're the most powerful pack in the South.

Several millennia ago, Scandinavian Viking wolf shifters sailed from the Old World and landed along the East Coast of what's now the United States. The six packs headed by best friends who sought new lands moved throughout the continent to form territories with ours settling here. We maintain close ties with our brethren through friendship, mating, and business. Plus, our Ruling Council gatherings keep us informed of happenings throughout the packs.

And even going that far and wide, I have yet to meet my fated mate. However, I will wait for her.

Hell, my wolf demands it as he gets agitated when he senses a she-wolf's burgeoning interest. Sure, he'll sit back while I fuck since it fills a need and doesn't equate to being mated. Wolf shifters—male and female—have strong sexual appetites. We don't have the same hang-ups as humans over casual sex, no sex before marriage, and whatever other bullshit they come up with. It's a part of our lives, just like eating or breathing. A need we won't suppress. Particularly with the built-up tension raging through my body. However, his pacing and snarls have increased recently, too.

So maybe Tag is on to something.

My *fated* mate.

A she-wolf whose scent I was born with teasing my nostrils. When she appears, I will recognize her by her distinct scent. No other will bear her uniqueness. Someday we will meet. I will give her my claiming bite, and we will have our mate bonding ceremony for all the clans to witness. I will make her mine forever.

The thought she may be in trouble makes my blood boil and my wolf snap his teeth, ears flat to his head. Our protective instinct on high alert.

So, I won't give up on finding my fated mate—or on us. No matter how many times my father bugs me about the need to bond with another. I'm no longer the teen who had to obey.

I am Alpha now.

"We're here, Alpha."

I glance up from my mobile screen and out the tinted window.

So focused on business emails, I didn't notice my driver

pull my Black Badge Rolls-Royce Cullinan into the driveway for Club Sol & Mani Miami. The flagship of six exclusive, luxury, members only BDSM clubs Larson Enterprises owns sits on Ocean Drive directly across from the Atlantic Ocean in a South Beach historic, beachfront gated mansion.

"Great, thank you, Cole," I respond. "I'll take it from here and will text when I'm ready to go home."

"Yes, Alpha. I'll get the door for you."

I wave him off and reach for the handle, only for the club's valet to open the door. A nod to Cole and a thanks in the form of a hundred to the young wolf shifter, and I stride to the scrolled wrought-iron and glass doors of the Spanish-style mansion. Laughter from members as they frolic in the mosaic-tiled pool within the sun-filled court-yard floats in the balmy evening air.

"Good evening, Alpha," the doorman says with a respectful bow of his head. I shake his hand and palm off another hundred. He thanks me as I move on.

"Hello, Alpha!" The two she-wolf greeters chorus cheer-fully as I walk through the opulent lobby to the elevators. Another two C-notes and I'm on the elevator headed to my personal suite.

Tonight, I'll play in privacy rather than amongst other members in Exhibition where demonstrations and perfor-mance rooms provide entertainment—or inspiration. Nor will the Dungeon do, despite my affinity for the spacious section devoted to public forms of BDSM play. Those not in the lifestyle may think it's a medieval dungeon for torture with the St. Andrew's Crosses, spanking benches, chains suspended from the ceiling, and more. To me, the pieces and assorted whips, floggers, canes, and implements are only to be expected.

The soft thrum of sensual music greets me as I step out of the elevator and into the hallway. The rhythm vibrates through my core as intended to amp arousal for what lies behind the closed doors of the eight private suites. Members can reserve them in advance should they prefer the same privacy I wish for tonight.

Each suite decorated by theme has various BDSM pieces, implements, and toys. A nice variety of options to choose from. However, my suite remains for my personal use only.

I press my palm against the plate by the door of the corner suite, and the locks disengage.

"Good evening, Alpha."

My head jerks up. What the fuck?! I allow no one in my space without my consent. My ice blue eyes adjust to the candlelit room. On my custom-built mahogany wood, king-size bed cornered by four thick carved posters and a brass lattice canopy with rings strategically attached sits a she-wolf from my pack. And not just any she-wolf. The sable-haired hellion.

"Melissa, what the fuck are you doing in my suite?!" I snarl as I stalk towards her.

She jerks back as though slapped but recovers quickly. Fully naked, she rises from the bed with the prowess of a wolf in hunt mode and slinks towards me. Amber eyes glow in the candlelight. She tosses her waist-length sable brown hair over her shoulders. Her sleek figure with high perky tits tipped by puckered rosy nipples, flat belly, narrow waist, slim hips, and long, toned legs would make any male salivate.

Not me.

Even though I planned to fuck her tonight—after I *invited* her to my suite—my stomach churns at the thought as my wolf growls low in his broad chest. He's not happy, nor am I.

Melissa is one of my regular sexual partners. We scratch the itch for each other from time to time. However, it's not like we're exclusive. Many a she-wolf join me for carnal pleasures. As Melissa has with other males. And I've made it clear I am not interested in bonding with her.

But after this stunt, this may very well be the last time I hookup with her. If she thinks she can enter my domain uninvited, she's confused. And I will speak with the club manager about her gaining unapproved access.

I have no intention of giving Melissa any ideas.

Not happening.

For one, Melissa thinks she's the alpha since the other male wolf shifters in our pack bow down to her beauty and succumb to her whims. I won't have it.

Not to mention she's a bully. Another trait I will not tolerate. I treat everyone in our pack with respect. They may not be my equal, but I don't make them feel less than.

And the most important reason... She's not my fated

mate. The only wolf shifter who will enter my domain as she pleases.

My wolf agrees with a flick of his feathery tail.

"Melissa, I have told you we fuck. Nothing more"—I raise my hand to stop her response—"You have no right to enter my personal suite without my permission. None. Get dressed. I will inform the club manager not to allow you entry ever again. This is it. Do you understand?"

She blinks, then her mouth opens.

I fold my arms over my chest and stand with feet spread far apart in a dominant manner as I pin her with an arctic gaze.

Naturally, Melissa glares back and mimics my stance as her eyes blaze golden fire.

"Jag—"

"Alpha! Alpha, Melissa. And do not forget it. We may have fucked. But you will respect me as your Alpha. Get. Dressed. And. Go. Now."

She lifts her chin in defiance, then reconsiders when I slap my sizable palm on my muscular thigh. Her eyes widen at the warning. Then she scurries to the chair and gathers her clothes to her flushed chest.

"Yes, Alpha!" She exclaims.

With a stern eye, I watch as she dresses quickly.

Melissa stops at the door and glances at me over her shoulder. Her oval-shaped face pinched with worry. She knows she took it too far this time.

"Sorry, Alpha," she whispers, then opens the door and leaves.

I sigh and sink onto the bed.

Well, there goes the idea of releasing tension. More just built up.

With his tongue hanging out from the side of his mouth, my wolf yips. Ice blue eyes gleam with mirth. It's as though he laughs at my misfortune.

I growl at him and slump back on the navy blue silk pillows. My thoughts drift to my conversation with Tag. Perhaps fate doesn't want me with another since my mate will appear soon. My eyes close on a sigh.

Where are you?

~

Click the Image Below or Visit books2read.com/u/ mZEL2e For Your Copy

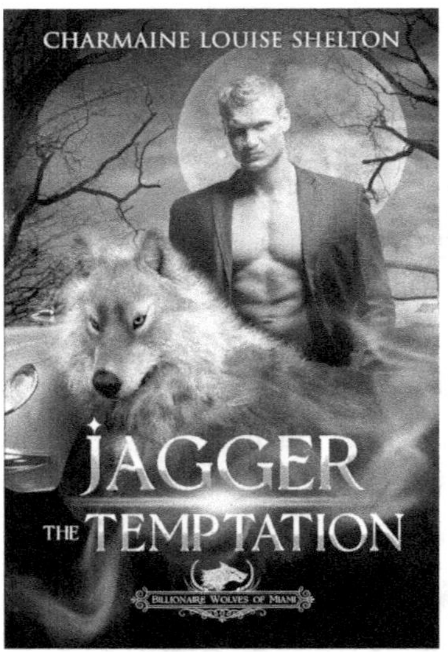

Jagger The Temptation: A Wolf Shifter Fated Mates
Paranormal Romance

NEXT IN SERIES VIGGO THE OBSESSION: A WOLF SHIFTER FATED MATES PARANORMAL ROMANCE

I'm the playboy prince who vowed it would never happen. Then it did. And she became my obsession.

Every female, she-wolf and human, wants a piece of me. So why should I choose only one? Unlike my brother—the leader of our pack, the Billionaire Wolves of Miami—and our best friends, I have zero interest in settling down with my fated mate. If she even exists.

But then Maya Alejandra Perez Garcia walks into my club.

I LOVE the life I made for myself in Miami, away from my controlling family in Venezuela. They allow me to leave until I turn twenty-five. Now, they demand I return to marry a man of their choosing, not mine. Before I go, I have one night to do as my heart wants. And it's Viggo

239

Larson, the sexy as sin man who watches me with smoldering eyes.

How could I know my steamy act of rebellion would result in a surprise and Viggo having one of his own?

Read **Viggo The Obsession** today.

Their steamy love story is a standalone in the sizzling Billionaire Wolves Series of interconnecting stories featuring wolf shifter fated mates romance. Get a glimpse of their dynamism in other books.

Click the Image Below or Visit books2read.com/u/ bwrDzG For Your Copy

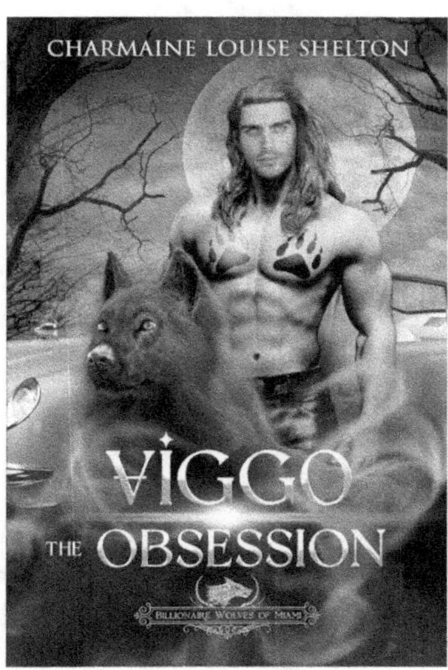

Viggo The Obsession: A Wolf Shifter Fated Mates
Paranormal Romance

WANT FREE BOOKS?

Want to know what happened to Jagger's best friend Dylan? Find out in *Dylan The Rogue: A Wolf Shifter Fated Mates Paranormal Romance* **your FREE Book!**

Click Cover Below or visit **bit.ly/ CLBooksDylanTheRogue** to subscribe to my newsletter for latest news and launches, books from my author friends, and sizzling reads in book promotions. Plus, start reading the steamy fated mates romance for bad boy wolf shifter Dylan.

A Trilogy of Desires Roger & Leonie Parts I-III

Series Extras

Series Playlist

STEELE INTERNATIONAL, INC. - JACKSON CORPORATION
A BILLIONAIRES ROMANCE SERIES CROSSOVER

Tempt My Desires Lachlan & Haley Part I

Tease My Desires Lachlan & Haley Part I

Grant My Desires Lachlan & Haley Part III

JACKSON CORPORATION

A BILLIONAIRES ROMANCE SERIES

Evoke My Desires Laurent & Yessenia Prequel

Light My Desires Laurent & Yessenia Part I

BILLIONAIRE WOLVES SERIES

WOLF SHIFTER FATED MATES PARANORMAL ROMANCE

MIAMI

Jagger The Awakening

(Available Exclusively for a Limited Time in Lunar Rising: A Collection of Paranormal Romance)

Dylan The Rogue

(Available Exclusively to Subscribers)

Jagger The Temptation

Rust The Rejected

Tag The Redemption

Viggo The Obsession

ABOUT CHARMAINE LOUISE SHELTON

Charmaine Louise Shelton loves a dominant Alpha hero—human, shifter, or vampire—as long as he's a billionaire and sexy as sin! Her romance novels take readers into the heroes' glitzy, glamorous, steamy worlds as they chase after independent women who unexpectedly capture their hearts. Want to experience some more? Download a free book at CharmaineLouiseBooks.com!

Find her at:
CharmaineLouiseBooks.com

Follow her on social media on your favorite channels below and **download your Free Book** at CharmaineLouise Books.com.

Fulfill Your Desires.

DEDICATION

To my awesome and dedicated beta readers and ARC Team, my amazing author friends, and this incredible community for their support.

And most of all to you, my loyal readers who love these couples as much as I do.

Thank you!

Cover Design: Murphy Wallace, Midnight Designs

Fulfill Your Desires.

xoxo

Charmaine Louise Shelton

www.ingramcontent.com/pod-product-compliance
Lightning Source LLC
Chambersburg PA
CBHW070447200726
48293CB00007B/2138